hex education

hex education

EMILY GOULD
&
ZAREEN JAFFERY

razOr
bill

Hex Education

RAZORBILL

Published by the Penguin Group
Penguin Young Readers Group
345 Hudson Street, New York, New York 10014, U.S.A.
Penguin Group (USA) Inc., 375 Hudson Street, New York, New York 10014, U.S.A.
Penguin Group (Canada), 90 Eglinton Avenue East, Suite 700, Toronto,
Ontario, Canada M4P 2Y3 (a division of Pearson Penguin Canada Inc.)
Penguin Books Ltd, 80 Strand, London WC2R 0RL, England
Penguin Ireland, 25 St Stephen's Green, Dublin 2, Ireland
(a division of Penguin Books Ltd)
Penguin Group (Australia), 250 Camberwell Road, Camberwell,
Victoria 3124, Australia (a division of Pearson Australia Group Pty Ltd)
Penguin Books India Pvt Ltd, 11 Community Centre, Panchsheel Park,
New Delhi – 110 017, India
Penguin Group (NZ), Cnr Airborne and Rosedale Roads,
Albany, Auckland 1310, New Zealand (a division of Pearson New Zealand Ltd)
Penguin Books (South Africa) (Pty) Ltd, 24 Sturdee Avenue,
Rosebank, Johannesburg 2196, South Africa

Penguin Books Ltd, Registered Offices: 80 Strand, London WC2R 0RL, England

10 9 8 7 6 5 4 3 2 1

Library of Congress Cataloging-in-Publication Data is available

Printed in the United States of America

hex education

1

It's been six hours, thirty-two minutes, and twenty-one endless seconds since the plane took off from LAX, which might not seem like such a long time to you. But then, you haven't spent it trapped in the company of Scott "Spooky" Stone and his lovely wife, Summer. The famous horror director and his costume designer/muse are quite possibly two of the most irritating people on earth, especially when they're in good moods. And today, they couldn't be more thrilled.

"There's the sign! Raven's Ridge scenic overlook!" Summer shouts to Spooky, who grins from ear to ear. "That means we're almost in Mythic! And *that* means you're almost home!"

Mythic, Massachusetts, as every horror fan worth his subscription to *Fangoria* magazine knows, is Spooky Stone's birthplace. According to all the guidebooks, this quaint hamlet is one of New England's most popular tourist destinations for visitors with an interest in witchcraft and the occult.

Believe me, Spooky and Summer are interested—interested

enough to respond to some kooky letter that said the town had been damaged by a recent bout of terrible storms this summer. Interested enough to consider the letter's request that they return to Mythic, bringing their Hollywood clout and cash with them. Interested enough to pack up all their belongings, sell a perfectly gorgeous house in Laurel Canyon, and move cross-country to try to help the town get back on its feet—and maybe shoot a historically inspired witch movie or two while they're at it.

Yeah, Spooky and Summer have it all figured out, and they couldn't be more psyched.

But there's just one small detail they've forgotten to take into consideration: me.

I'm Sophie Stone, Spooky and Summer's fourteen-year-old daughter. If you've been following Spooky's career, you're probably thinking, *Oh yeah! The baby in the spider-print onesie that Summer brought to the premiere of* Shriek 3. You probably figure that I grew up goth, with dyed-black, Morticia-center-parted hair like my mother's, and that I'm ready to step into my father's signature Doc Martens and direct my first gore-filled featurette any day now.

You'd be wrong, wrong, wrongity wrong wrong wrong.

"Sophie, look out the window to your left," says my dad. "We're just passing Poisoned Pond. It's called that because of all the witches who cursed it before they were drowned there back in colonial times!"

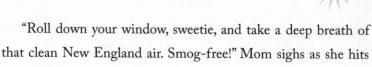

"Roll down your window, sweetie, and take a deep breath of that clean New England air. Smog-free!" Mom sighs as she hits the window button for me.

"They weren't really witches; they were just mean old ladies. Everyone with a grade school education knows that," I say, rolling (a) my eyes and (b) the window back up.

"Oh, quit being such a pile of wet blankets, Soph. You're acting like you don't have any interest in learning about the town your ancestors are from!"

"Um, I don't, actually," I say. "Can we please, please start heading back to LA now? I have this 'life' thing I said I'd go to."

Mom turns around in her seat, her pile of silver necklaces clanking like wind chimes, and fixes me with her most sincere gaze. "Sophie, I know this isn't easy for you—"

"You do?" I interrupt. "Which part do you think is the least 'easy'—starting high school at a new school in a town so tiny that everyone has probably had the same friends since birth? Or the fact that said tiny town is just as obsessed with the macabre as my freak show parents?"

Mom's trying to maintain her cool, but I can tell that the "freak show" thing struck a nerve. The vein in the middle of her forehead is now gently twitching. Still, she manages to spit out some more textbook parenting before turning back to face the road.

"Give Mythic a chance, Sophie. Having a closed mind never made anyone happy."

We drive for another half mile or so in silence. The scenery on either side of the winding road rushes past us in a blur of crumbling farmhouses and tall, forbidding pines. I shut my eyes and imagine palms and eucalyptus, the sweet smell of jacaranda. I want more than anything to be back home. But when I open my eyes, I'm still on the opposite coast, where I already know that nothing is going to make sense.

Back in LA, I fit in. My parents' weirdnesses—and their celebrity—barely raised an eyebrow in a town full of richer, odder stars. As long as I made sure there was no black in *my* wardrobe, it wasn't that hard to blend.

But Mythic is my dad's hometown, and he's moving back for the specific purpose of being its valiant savior from whatever. Like it or not, I'm going to be outed as his offspring as soon as anyone takes attendance. And sometimes, you *don't* want to go where everybody knows your name. Because everyone in Mythic will expect me to be Spooky Junior, and the truth is, I just don't have a skeleton-loving bone in my body.

You'd think that fourteen years would be enough time for my parents to wrap their minds around this.

Um, *no*.

"So tell us more about the history of your town, hon," Mom says. "Maybe hearing more about her ancestors will help Sophie get more excited about Mythic."

Sure, and maybe *Disemboweler IV* will get nominated for an Oscar.

"That's a great idea, sweetie," my dad says. He glances at me in the rearview. "Maybe we can start to hash out the plot of *The Witches of Mythic* at the same time. So here's the basic gist: During colonial times, witches fled from nearby Salem and founded this town. They planned to live away from their oppressors in a witch-only society, but they ran into a problem: the religious leaders in the surrounding towns wouldn't leave them alone. Eventually, those leaders got together and turned on the witches, massacring them. You know, in the pond."

"Oh, that's so perfect!" crows Mom. "We can totally dramatize that part, with the slaughter, in the movie!"

"Well, the story doesn't end there," says Dad. "The witches may not have survived, but their magic did. And few generations later, a new coven was born. These witches found each other and realized that they needed to conceal their powers or risk meeting their ancestors' fate. So they hid their magic—tamped it down, never used it unless it was really necessary."

"Oh, come *on*. You're talking like there's such a thing as witches—like there's such a thing as magic!" I say.

My dad totally ignores me, caught up in his tale. "They would've been able to escape detection, too, except for one thing. One of those witches decided to use her power for evil. What happened next is a little fuzzy. We don't know exactly what occurred, but two centuries ago, fierce winds and mysterious fires destroyed much of the town."

I grip the driver's headrest and pull myself forward. "Storms? Yeah, Dad, those happen sometimes."

But I can see there is no getting through to him. He has that faraway look in his eye. He might as well be on some other planet.

"Scott, honey, do you think that in the movie, the town should still be full of true believers who are just hanging out, waiting for the next coven to be born? Or is that not believable?" asks my mom.

"I'm thinking it strains credulity a bit, honey," he replies. "Plus, it makes the shock less intense when the witches do appear."

"That's exactly what I was thinking," Mom coos, leaning over to plant a kiss on my father's cheek.

"Hey! Eyes on the *road*, guys!" I snap. A car crash is the only thing that could make my life worse at this point.

Dad looks up. "Oh. Thanks, Soph! I almost missed the turn-off for Raven's Ridge!" He pulls the car off the highway and soon we're squealing to a halt at the scenic overlook. "Grab my binoculars!"

As I step out of the car, my cute shoes are immediately covered in Massachusetts mud. Grumbling under my breath, I follow Mom and Dad to the rocky ledge.

We can see the whole town from here, and even though I wasn't expecting much, I'm still disappointed. For one thing, Mythic is even tinier than I'd imagined. A few main streets surround a central square, which itself is surrounded by a looser ring

of outlying roads lined with tall pines and big houses built on lots of forested land.

The major buildings—church, post office, town hall types of things—are all tall, dark, ornate structures, built of solid gray limestone studded with peaks and spires. There is a lot of gray and brown going on in the architecture. Mythic looks like some kind of twisted theme park. Gothland. Horror World. And Mom and Dad look like little kids about to get on the best ride.

Weird thing, though, is that looking out over the town, I get this sharp feeling of déjà vu. Is this the kind of thing that happens to *all* kids when they visit the place where one of their parents was raised? Is Mythic, like, imprinted in the most primitive part of my brain? I shudder at the thought.

We never came out here when I was growing up, because my dad's parents retired to Boca the second he made it big. Looking around this place, I can't say I blame them. Grandpa and Gran have a pretty sweet beach house there.

There are no sunny beaches in Mythic, though. In the far distance, beyond the acres of brush, I can see a choppy, inky black ocean. Big, dark clouds swirl above the waves, blowing in from the shore.

Dad breaks my gloomy contemplation by spouting some particularly crazy talk. "When shall we three meet again? In thunder, lightning, or in rain?"

"Uh, we'll probably meet every single day, Dad. We are unfortunately related." I scrutinize my father, wondering whether his

tiny brain has imploded from happiness. Then I realize he's reading the inscription on the base of a statue.

A statue of . . . *witches.*

Ugh. Dad's right—it *is* like we've stumbled onto the set of
one of his own movies.

Just to our right, a bronze trio of unkempt ladies in tattered,
dumpy dresses stands clustered around a bronze cauldron, with
expressions on their statue faces that I can really only describe
as . . . well . . . *wicked.*

"When the hurly-burly's done, when the battle's lost and
won . . ." Dad continues, his voice actually trembling with excitement, ". . . that will be ere the set of sun."

"Those are the Weird Sisters," Mom explains. "The witches
from *Macbeth.*"

"The statue was erected by the first coven. The people of
Mythic believe these ladies watch over the town. Quite a depar-
ture from the Hollywood sign, huh, Soph?" Dad smirks.

I swear, sometimes I think they actually enjoy tormenting me.

While my parents wander back toward the car, gushing about
how fascinating it all is, I take a surreptitious kick at the statue.
Weird Sisters, my butt. The inscription on the base of the statue
might as well read WELCOME TO MYTHIC. POPULATION: LAME. I
give the stone another kick for good measure—and that's when
things take a turn for the truly freakish.

My toe is immediately shot through with a sharp pain that
travels all the way up my calf, to the top of my leg. This isn't any

ordinary toe stub. This is strange, vibrating, never-before agony.

I double over, gripping the base of the statue, as the pain crawls up my back. It reaches my neck and explodes into the worst headache I've ever had.

"Sophie, honey, come on!" my dad calls from the car. Clearly, neither one of my parents has witnessed my strange attack. They've probably been too busy sucking face, or plotting their witch movie, or both.

Lucky for them, the pain disappears as quickly as it came. I release my death grip on the statue's base, shake my head to clear it, and shuffle slowly back to the car.

It's official: I am not feeling Mythic. Not one little bit.

2

As soon as we arrive at our new house—which, almost need-
less to say, is a Victorian of the "oh, the big old house at the
end of the street? No one ever goes up there. Rumor has it it's
haunted by an evil spirit that sucks the marrow out of innocent
teenagers' bones" variety—Mom and Dad busy themselves
with domestic chores. As they deliberate over what shade of
red will suit the dining room's black-lacquered moldings best
and yell at the movers for disturbing all the "gorgeous" cob-
webs, I head upstairs to hole up in my (gloomy, horrible) tur-
ret bedroom.

But eventually, Mom remembers the fact of my existence.
This happens sometimes, unfortunately.

"Knock, knock!" she says as she walks in. She never actually
knocks. Annoying thing about her number ten billion and one.
There's a little slip of orange paper in her black-nailed hand, and
she hands it to me.

"I thought you might want to use one of these coupons when

you head into town later," she says. "A bunch of them came in the welcome package that Ms. Lerner left for us."

My mother's statement brings up a few questions. Like, "Go into town, are you crazy?" and, "Coupon for what, a new life? " Eventually, I decide to just go for the straightforward one. "Who's Ms. Lerner?"

Mom rolls her heavily-eyelinered eyes. "Remember, honey? The letter Daddy got? The reason we're here?"

It sort of comes back to me. Some old biddy on the board of the Mythic Historical Society who'd been the one to reach out to Dad about moving here to help repair the damaged town. Right, whatever. I mean, if Dad's last three movies hadn't been complete flops, I'm guessing that letter would have gotten the pre-signed form response sent out to all Spooky Stone fans. But noooo, Dad wanted to be an altruist *and* return to his roots. Like moving to this town is going to somehow help his career. But everyone knows that once you leave LA you're, like, off the movie map, literally and figuratively.

I glance down at the coupon my mom hands me.

Ye Olde Strange Brews Coffee Shoppe

Half-priced Spooky Scone with purchase of any beverage

10% of proceeds are donated to the Save Mythic Fund

Mom giggles. "Spooky Scone! That's a new one. Tell me how they are, okay?"

"I hate to break this to you, Mom, but I'm not really that interested in . . ." I look down at the flyer. "Ye Olde Strange Brews

Coffee Shoppe. I mean, seriously, Strange Brews? I don't want to get turned into a toad by a latte."

Mom just keeps grinning. "That's funny, Soph! I'm glad you're getting into the spirit of things. Ha, the *spirit* of things!"

Now it's my turn to roll my eyes. "Earth to Summer. I'm not going, okay? I am not interested in anything about Gothville, USA. I'm just going to sit here in my room until you come to your senses and send me back to LA."

"Well, Soph, not that this should matter, but your dad is pretty beloved in this town. I'm guessing that's going to make you extra popular with the kids. And being popular can be a lot of fun . . ."

I can tell by her dreamy expression Mom is reliving the glory days of being prom queen in '86. Pink pouffy sleeves, gravity-defying bangs, un-ironic blue eye shadow. Scarier than any movie my dad could dream up.

". . . but you have to make sure they are your friends for the right reasons."

"Whatevs," I say. "Any crazy who wants to be friends with me because they think that scene in *Death by Design* where blood spews out of the architect's every orifice is cool can just crawl back into whatever gothy cave they came out of."

Summer's crimson grin crumples at this and she launches into a lecture about how I'm here and had better get used to it (take one hundred of this scene).

While she blah blah blahs, I go to my happy place. Well, okay, my not-miserable place: I imagine that I'm starting school tomorrow, not in some godforsaken gothic hamlet, but at comfy old Rancho Calabasas Junior High School of the Arts. I imagine myself back in eighth grade, at the decently cool table in the cafeteria, sitting with my lunch buddies Jenny, Celeste, and Alexa. They're all applying lip gloss and talking about who looks hot today. Oh, Jenny and Celeste and Alexa! Not the brightest lightbulbs on the Christmas tree, but still, I miss them.

I'm sure one or the other of them will call me soon.

I tune back into the momologue just in just in time to catch her saying, "Suit yourself, Soph. But trust me, nothing is as bad as you think. In a couple of weeks you'll start loving it here."

I snort. Not pretty, but it's the only thing left to say.

"Okay, I can't be around this negative energy anymore," Mom announces, betraying her Californian roots. Then she turns on her (spiked, black vinyl) heel and exits, finally leaving me alone.

I'm relieved. And then, a few seconds later, I start to feel kind of crappy. It's not like there's anything to do in my room except unpack, which obviously has less than zero appeal. I look out my window, at the so-called beach. It's desolate and rocky and probably has a lot of prickly dune grasses and biting flies and seaweed, but I guess I could still drag a towel out there and tan. If the sun ever came out.

I rest my head against the cool glass of the windowpane. *I want out of here,* I think, closing my eyes. I take a deep breath and stand back. That's when I see a small scratch on the window.

Huh. I trace the three-inch length of it with my finger. How weird I didn't notice that before. As I'm staring at it, another one appears, and a sharp pain pierces my skull as I examine it. This time, the scratch looks more like a crack, and it's a lot longer. Before I know it, dozens more are sprouting out from each side of the windowpane. I back away from the window just as the glass falls to the ground with a crash.

Oh no, I think. *Not again.*

3

"Mom!" I yell out. "This place is totally falling apart!"

My mom walks in, and I motion at the now-empty space where a window used to be. "It cracked right in front of me. I don't even want to know how old glass has to be to do that," I say. "Oh lighten up, Sophie," she says. "Comes with the territory."

I leave my mom cheerily cleaning up the mess, grab the coupon for Strange Brews, and head downstairs. My mind is racing. The thing is—this isn't the first time something like this has happened to me. . . .

This summer, when my friends and I were hanging out at my house and my mom wouldn't let me leave with them to go to the new dessert bar in West Hollywood? I meanly wished that my friends wouldn't get to go either. At that moment, right before my eyes, all the tires on Alexa's junior-in-high-school boyfriend's car blew out.

I thought it was just a coincidence. A really funny and perfect coincidence, but still . . .

And then on the fourth of July, Jenny was having a party at her beach house in Malibu. This girl Talia, who I *hate*, was also there and wouldn't stop talking about how her dad took her to the *Vanity Fair* Oscar party (which my dad has yet to be invited to, and she knows it).

All I wanted was for her to shut up. And when she took her next sip of soda, that's exactly what happened. First she started coughing. Then she grabbed her throat, like she was choking.

Later, I found out she'd had some sort of allergic reaction. But *still* . . .

Or what about the time I went to visit my dad on the set of a movie his friend was producing? They were shooting at this old hotel that hadn't been open since the 1960s. The coolest thing about the place was this ginormous fountain in the center—a fountain that hadn't worked in decades. My dad was giving me a tour of the place, and I thought, *How nice it would be if that fountain was running.*

Guess what happened next? That's right: waterworks.

My dad thought it was some kind of movie miracle. *But. Still.*

Even weirder is that each time these things happened, I got a headache right before. Just like I did at the window . . .

But there's no way I was responsible for any of those things, right? They were just coincidences. Random acts of weirdness.

I decide to do what I do best and ignore it. Time to brave the wilds of Mythic's Main Street. I'm betting that all the stores on it have some variation of *Ye* or *Olde* or *Shoppe* in their names. But I guess I could check them out, just to make sure there's nothing in them that could possibly make the next four years of my life less painful.

Maybe I could take up some kind of handicraft, like knitting or whittling. They probably sell supplies for one or the other at Ye Olde Yarn and Whittling Supply Shoppe.

Before I leave, I change out of my lounging-around outfit into a cute white tennis skirt, moccasins, and a washed-soft old T-shirt with a faded heart pattern on it. I grab my sunglasses from my purse, slide them on, and jog toward the stairs. In the hallway, I run into a tall, lumpen "ghost" in a cobweb-strewn shroud.

"Boo!" it shouts in Dad's unmistakable voice. I don't even do him the courtesy of pretending to be scared. The man cannot resist a dumb prank. "Spooky Stone's overgrown-child quality is what has made him a legendary horror director," according to *Movie Massacre Monthly*. Uh, right. His shroud— okay, it's a bedsheet—is sheer, so I can see the blissed-out grin on his face.

"There she is!" Dad cheers. "I bet you're just about to come and help me install a black light in the den!"

Wordlessly, I flip up my shades so that he can see the look I'm giving him.

From just behind me comes a strange keening noise. "Is there another 'spectral presence' I should be aware of, Dad?" I ask, willing myself not to turn in the direction of the yowl.

Dad chuckles. "You haven't met Crispy yet, I take it."

I've just opened my mouth to ask what the hell he's talking about when some *thing* brushes up against my leg. This time, I jump and scream, prompting my dad to laugh hysterically at what I now see is a midnight black cat running full steam out the open front door.

When I manage to catch my breath, I ask, "Crispy?"

"Your mom found him wandering around the yard. She's adopted him."

My mouth opens. Then closes. I can't come up with any response more appropriate than, "I'm leaving."

"Well, have a great time! Just be sure you make it back in time for dinner—Mom is making mushroom-squash casserole!" He whistles a happy little tune to himself as he sweeps off down the hallway, his shroud trailing behind him.

"What. Evs." I growl; then I feel a momentary pang of guilt when he shoots me a hurt look over his shoulder. It must be fun on the bizarro planet where he lives, and here am I, hovering like a perpetual rain cloud over his and Mom's parade.

But I've been uprooted from my life and forced to start over in a strange little seaside town that's obsessed with the macabre. I'm entitled to be a little attitudinal, right?

Since it's a bit of a trek to get into town, I hop on an old red bike that's rusting by the front gate. It seems to have come with the house. It squeaks when I brake, and it's far from a glamorous ride, but it'll get me where I'm going. When I reach the end of our long, tree-lined driveway, I turn back and look at my new home.

The dormer windows, complete with their old-fashioned pull-down tasseled shades, stare back at me like hooded, evil eyes. I watch Crispy preparing to curl up on one of the downstairs windowsills. He arches his back for a moment, and *ugh*, the clichéd creepiness of our new home is complete. Then he settles down and starts licking himself in his manly area, which is considerably less creepy. Well, creepy in a different way.

The wind is fairly wild today, blowing my ponytail in a straight line behind me and sending dry leaves flying at my face. It's still overcast, and a slight drizzle begins pattering down as I make my way closer to the town. I pass a bunch of houses that look just about as haunted as mine. Tall, scraggly pine trees line the road, some with split trunks and broken-off branches. Huh. Guess those storms we're here to save the town from are no joke after all.

Some of the houses already have Halloween decorations up, which seems (a) redundant and (b) premature, considering that it's, um, *August*. Still, I guess it's what you'd expect from a town whose sole claim to fame is that some historical witches lived (and died) here.

As I get closer to the center of town, the broken trees become more predominant, and the houses have broken windows and big patches of missing shingles. It makes them look like beaten faces, with missing teeth and black eyes, and I get another creepy chill.

But in spite of everything, it's nice to get some fresh air, and by the time I get to Main Street (well, at least it's not Ye Maine Streete), I've worked myself into a slightly less foul mood. I lean my bike up against a wrought-iron street lamp and dismount.

The damage here in what could charitably be called Mythic's downtown is much more obvious. Shingles litter the sidewalk, and cracks in the foundations of the low-slung brick buildings creep all the way up to their sagging eaves. Gingerbread trim hangs precariously from a tack. Even some of the roadway's weathered paving stones have been overturned. It seems like the town is basically crumbling around its inhabitants' ears.

And in spite of everything, I feel a prickle of . . . is it excitement? Maybe just curiosity. It kind of feels like the weird déjà vu I got near the witch statue.

Well, anything's better than bleak, life-is-over misery, I guess.

At the center of the block I spot a hanging sign—a cauldron shaped like a coffee mug. This must be Strange Brews, home of the "Spooky Scone." Striding determinedly through the door and into the quaint atmosphere, I lean into the counter and deliver my usual Coffee Bean & Tea Leaf order to a barista, who has his back turned toward me:

"Tallhalfcafsoypeppermintmocha. Oh, and extra foam, please?"

The guy turns around. And: whoa.

Mythic's approval rating skyrockets when he smiles, squinting at me from behind his floppy blond hair. He's tall, but looks to be about my age. His name tag reads LINC MONTGOMERY. The soap star name makes me feel like somebody might be messing with me—I mean, *Linc Montgomery*? His athletic build allows him to totally pull off a poly-blend coffee brown polo. His killer blue eyes match his apron perfectly. The expression in said eyes, however, is completely befuddled.

"I'm sorry, but we just have regular and decaf."

Suddenly, I feel really stupid about wearing sunglasses indoors. I try to remove them subtly. "So . . . you don't have espresso drinks here?"

Linc—*Linc?*—smiles kindly at me, and I inwardly swoon.

"You must be new in town," he says. "We have an espresso machine, but it's on the fritz. Um, again."

I return Linc's smile and silently promise to give Mythic the benefit of the doubt—for now.

"Well, regular coffee then, please," I tell him.

He turns to fill my order. "So, have you been to the museum already?"

I blink. A museum? This dinky little burg has an art museum?

"Oh yeah, I was really impressed with the collection," I bluff. "Definitely some beautiful pieces."

Linc gives me a bemused look. "Have you been to a lot of witchcraft museums *besides* the Mythic Historical Society?"

I'm glad I haven't gotten my coffee yet, because I'd probably be spitting it out in horror. Talk about sending the wrong message!

"Nonono. I don't know anything about that stuff," I say, back-pedaling. "I just was so impressed because—because I'd never seen any Wiccan artifacts before." I pause. *"Ever!"*

I wait for Linc to back away slowly and call the men in white suits to come and take me away. But instead, he smiles and tact-fully changes the subject. "So are you sticking around in Mythic for a while, or are you just here on a day trip?" he asks as he turns back to the counter.

"My family just moved here, actually. I'm about to start school at Mythic High. Do you go there?"

"I will. . . . I'm going to be a freshman," he says.

"Me too!" I say, trying (maybe not hard enough) to keep the excitement out of my voice. "I'm Sophie, by the way."

Linc leans toward me with squinched-up eyebrows, as if he's about to ask a difficult question. A moment passes, then another.

"So, Sophie. Do you want . . ."

My brain begins to buzz. Oh my God. Is he going to ask me out? Wait until I tell Alexa/Jenny/Celeste that I got a date before school even started!

"Sure!" I squeak.

". . . milk?" Linc finishes.

I close my eyes. My face, undoubtedly, turns purple. I nod silently.

He just smiles, though, and makes to top off my cup. Then he gives the carton a discouraged shake. "Pudder!" he shouts.

Another brown-uniformed dude appears from the back. "Yes, Linc?" he says, already wincing.

Linc holds the carton aloft. "Milk, Pudder. We're out."

"Sure thing," says . . . Pudder. I immediately see the reason for the humiliating nickname: the tag on his shirt reads PAUL PUD-NOWSKI.

I hate to say it, but he kind of *looks* like a Paul Pudnowski. Where Linc has muscles, Paul has posture issues. And while Linc's baby blues are the stuff dreams are made of, Paul's eyes are the stuff thick glasses are made to correct the vision of.

But who am I to talk? I'm the new kid. Judge not, lest ye be, and all that.

Linc gives me an apologetic glance, then opens his mouth to speak. The sound of a little chime stops him. The front door of the coffee shop swings open, and a waft of cotton-candyish perfume fills the air. Looking at something directly behind me, Linc wordlessly deposits my paper cup of coffee on the counter and heads into the back room of the café.

"Emergency, Pudder. Coreymergency," I hear him say in a muffled voice. A second later, Paul emerges from the back.

And then something very blond is swishing past me, up to the counter.

"Hi, Corey. Linc's not here."

"Latte, skim, no foam. I mean not even a *tiny little bit* of foam," the blonde demands.

"Well, the espresso machine is still broken. And actually,

there's someone . . . um . . . there's another customer ahead of you? Who I haven't rung up yet? Sorry?"

There's a cold silence, during which I start to feel very, very sorry for Paul Pudnowski.

The blonde turns around and faces me. She also looks about my age, but her immaculate, American Girl doll–style ringlets belong on someone much older. Her outfit is head-to-toe pink, to match her nauseating perfume. Her eyes are steely gray and mean. I catch myself beginning to back toward the door.

"You don't mind, do you." It's not really a question. I make some kind of gesture with my head, and Corey turns back to Paul. "She doesn't mind. Give me a small black coffee. That espresso machine better be fixed next time I'm in here. And Linc better say hi to me next time." As Paul hurriedly fills her order, Corey cranes her head toward the back room. *"Hi, sweetie!"* she shouts. Then she plunks a couple of quarters down on the counter and is gone as quickly as she arrived.

I look at the coins, then back up at Paul Pudnowski, who is staring sadly down at the straw dispenser.

"Fifty cents! So this town has something going for it after all," I say, because I have to say something.

Paul smiles a definite "A girl! Is being nice! To me!" smile. "Well, Corey sort of gets the psychopath discount. It's actually supposed to be seventy-five cents—but I'm way too scared to tell her about the price increase."

"Yeah, she's scarier than every Halloween decoration I've seen today."

Paul shrugs. "Guess you can act however you want when you're Corey Upton."

"Really?" I frown in confusion. "Why?"

"Her mom and dad are the most powerful people around. They're rich, and Mrs. Upton likes to brag about how her family goes back to Mythic's original settlers."

"Like anyone cares?"

"You'd be surprised," Paul tells me. "Pretty much anything the Uptons say in this town goes."

An awkward silence descends, and I decide it's probably a good idea to change the subject. "Sooo, seventy-five cents is still pretty cheap—so yeah, score one for Mythic."

Paul leans his elbows on the counter. "Well, things are cheap in rural Guatemala too, although I think they probably have a slightly more boring nightlife."

"I was never one for the nightlife anyhow," I say, playing along. "Maybe we should move to Guatemala. I could learn to love eating capybara."

"Capybara . . . nice." Paul nods appreciatively. "Referencing the local fauna. I see I'm playing out of my league. Before you come to your senses about this whole thing, I'll book our tickets."

He turns to Linc, who's finally reemerged from the back room. "Hey, can you cover my shifts? I just decided to move to South America with some girl whose name I don't even know."

"That's Sophie," Linc says. "And keep dreaming. Girls can't tolerate you long enough to walk across the street with you." He absentmindedly punches Paul on the arm as he walks past.

"That hurts, man," Paul says. He places a hand over his heart to ease his mock pain. "It hurts me, deep inside."

"But speaking of covering shifts," Linc continues, lowering his voice so that I almost can't catch what he's saying, "I need, like, fifteen minutes—just gonna go out front. Girl issues. You're being upgraded from busboy while I'm out, Pudder."

Paul barely winces at the name, then pastes on a bland smile. "Be my guest. I've got everything under control here." He smiles at me, grabs the carton of milk, and pours the contents into my coffee cup with a dorky flourish. Linc brushes past me on his way toward the door, cell already out of his pocket.

But then, suddenly, he turns around and faces us.

"Pudder, did you even ask if she wanted sugar?" Paul shakes his head, and Linc strides back toward me. Grabbing a shaker, he pours a scant spoonful into my cup. "Not too sweet," he says under his breath, then flicks his eyes toward my face for what can't be more than a second.

Still, my breath stops. Are we having, like, a moment?

Or am I delusional?

Or, option (c): am I just insanely clumsy? Because as Linc turns back to leave, I nearly knock my cup of steaming hot, milky, not-too-sweet coffee onto the stack of newspapers sitting on the counter.

I raise my hand to grab the cup before it spills, but as it's teetering on the edge of falling over, it stops, mid-tip. I move my hand closer, and the cup moves back into its natural standing position.

I gasp. What *was* that? How did my coffee just stop—in midair?

Is it possible that Mythic, Massachusetts, has invented spill-proof cups? This place is so chock-full of hokey crap—like the plastic tarantulas hanging from the ceiling—that it isn't hard to imagine.

I look up to see if anyone has noticed this latest weirdo episode, but Linc is almost out the door, and Paul has his head stuck in a copy of the *Mythic Gazette*. It would probably be good to bone up on my new community, so I grab a *Gazette* and fold it under my arm just as Paul looks back up at me.

"Hey! You're Spooky Stone's daughter!"

I wince. "You know? How?"

He flips the paper around and points to the bottom half of the front page. The title of the article? "The Return of Spooky."

There's an accompanying picture of my dad wearing his mid-eighties signature all-black ensemble. My mom, looking gorgeous in a black sheath dress. And me—in all my spider-print onesie glory. Beneath *that* photo, my eighth-grade class portrait. So much for blending in.

"I have to ask"—Paul leans in—"are you really into horror movies? Because I am."

"Sorry to disappoint you, but no, I'm not. I'm not into all this witchy whatnot either." I shrug. "I think maybe I'm going to have a hard time fitting in here."

"Huh, I hear you! And you know, actually, I think I might branch out film-wise. Maybe explore some French New Wave. Maybe we could watch something sometime?"

"Maybe," I say noncommittally. I'm being a snob, I realize, but I do have hesitations about befriending a horror-movie lover whose nickname is "Pudder."

I mean, he *is* the first non–family member I've had a real conversation with since stepping off the plane . . . but step one of not being a social outcast is: avoid befriending social outcasts.

As my luck would have it, the barely noticeable drizzle becomes a downpour the moment I step out of Strange Brews and onto the sidewalk outside. Wow, not only does this town have great amenities, it has great weather too! Too bad I brought exactly zero umbrellas with me.

That was a bad move. Come to think of it, so was wearing an all-white outfit and Powerpuff Girls–patterned underwear.

Within about thirty seconds, I'm drenched and semi-translucent and definitely, *definitely* not about to go back into the coffee shop.

I look up and down Mythic's decrepit main drag. Maybe there's some kind of boutique where a kindly old woman will provide me with a hand-knitted poncho that I can ride home in. Or a general store where I can buy some trash bags that I can improvise into some kind of raincoat?

But as far as the eye can see, there are nothing but dusty, ill-marked storefronts that don't seem like they've been open for decades. I do see the museum Linc was talking about, though. And right next to it, is the Mythic Historical Society Gifte Shoppe.

Through the dusty panes of its tiny front window, I see that the lights are on.

I breathe a sigh of relief. Help me, Gifte Shoppe. You're my only hope.

The heavy wooden door creaks as I shove it open. It takes my rain-clouded eyes a second to adjust to the gloom, but when they do, I see racks and racks of souvenir tchotchkes, broomsticks and pointy hats, chintzy jewelry with lots of black and purple stones, and a bunch of books with black cats, spiders, and the word *lore* featured on the covers. There's also a clothes rack toward the back— and no one standing behind the cash register, for the moment at least. Without wasting a moment, I grab the first garment I see—a long black velvet dress with a lace-up bodice that would no doubt flatter my bosom, if I had one—and head for the fitting room. While I'm stowing my former outfit in my fortunately commodious handbag, I hear strains of the Cure wafting through the store. I emerge just as the salesgirl pokes her head out of the back room.

"Cursed CD player keeps skipping," she mutters.

Whoa, she actually said *cursed*. Like, with two syllables: *Curse. Ed.* Her eyeliner extends almost to her hairline, her skin is powdered corpse white, and her dyed-black hair matches her black-on-black-on-black outfit (complete with black fingerless gloves—nice touch). She's also sporting a cluster of painful-looking

piercings in her lower lip and eyebrow. And her nose hasn't escaped
unscathed—it has a tiny semiprecious zit in the corner of its left
nostril. She smiles when she looks up and sees me in my velvet
Renaissance faire regalia.

Oh, great. She thinks I'm some sort of kyndred spyryt, no
doubt. If she only knew about my dad, she'd probably try to bind
us as blood sisters or something.

"By the goddess, that dress looks awesome on you! Do you
have a special occasion coming up?" she says, stroking one of its
hideous belled cuffs.

I roll my eyes. "Um, yeah, a really important crypt warm-
ing next weekend. All the cool werewolves and vampires will be
there," I say with a sneer. I catch a glimpse of myself in the mirror
and realize that it's not a very becoming expression. A little more
reflection results in the conclusion that I'm being kind of awful
for no reason, and I promptly start to feel bad about it. Way to
make friends, Sophie.

"Look. I'm sorry, that was rude, especially if you take this
stuff"—I gesture at the gewgaws and knickknacks—"seriously.
I'm just having, like, a really bad day. I'm Sophie, by the way—
what's your name?"

Glowering silently, the sales goth points at a pewter-edged
name tag. Spelled out in pseudo-runes is the word ESMERALDA.

"Okay, well, I'll just pay for this dress and be on my way?" I
say, smiling desperately.

She gives me a forced half smile and rings up the dress, which

is pretty expensive, especially considering the fact that it's a glori-
fied Halloween costume and I'll only be wearing it for the ride
home. Forcing a smile of my own, I hand over my Visa.

"I'll need to see some photo ID." She smirks.

I scrounge through my purse, glad that I haven't yet con-
signed my ID from my old junior high to my keepsake collection.
Esmeralda holds it to the light.

"Sophie Stone from California—I should have guessed," she
mutters under her breath.

I snatch the card back from her, my friendly vibe dissipating
into the air like the clouds of incense that clog the store. "What's
that supposed to mean?"

Esmeralda just shoots me what I'm assuming she thinks is
a mysterious smirk, which ends up looking all deranged clown
thanks to her makeup. "Nothing. Just, like, come again, duuude,"
she says in a ridiculous pseudo-Californian voice.

As I leave the store, her laughter follows me. It's cut off by the
groaning front door, which slams shut behind me.

Well, that *could have gone better,* I think as I hike up my goth-
tacular gown and hop on my bike. The rain is still coming down
as I pedal home, but at least I'm no longer wearing the incredible
disappearing outfit.

And on the bright side, the first day of school has to be a
cakewalk compared to my introduction to Mythic.

I mean really, it *has to be.*

Not on my best days am I a morning person. And today, I am grumpier than one of those barking old dudes that my dad insists on watching on CNN.

Since my reconnaissance mission yesterday as to the scene in Mythic resulted only in the resolution not to sport any white clothing, I carefully planned my first-day-of-high-school outfit.

I picked a comfy Marc by Marc Jacobs oversized hoodie with a tank underneath in case it gets hot. For my lower half, I chose a mini made out of a pair of old Levi's and my perfect vintage cowboy boots. I decided that it was the perfect look-how-hard-I'm-not-trying ensemble, but not before I'd tried at least a dozen different variations of said ensemble. (I'm ridiculous, I know.)

The all-knowing mirror reveals, er, all. My outfit is perfect. Or . . . well thought out at least. My brown hair is shiny and Redken super-Str8, thanks to an early-morning blow-dry. My lips are MAC lip-glossy, my lashes Voluminous.

In a last-minute burst of inspiration, I paw through the

still-not-unpacked mess that's lying around my room. It takes a minute before I find it— the little hinged box that contains Alexa's goodbye present.

I open it and pull out a pair of floppy little baggies that slither around in my fingers.

"They're *out*plants," Alexa told me when I first opened the package, back in LA. "You just stick them inside your bra. Think about it, Soph—you've never met these people before. There's no reason for them to know that you're flat as a pancake! Besides, success in a new social environment is about not being afraid of taking opportunities. I read that in my dad's girlfriend's *Cosmo*."

That's Alexa for you. Always there with the tact. But I even miss that about my old life.

God, I don't just miss that. I miss the smog. I miss the traffic on the 101. I miss *everything*.

Sigh.

I snuggle the cold silicone baggies safely into my bra, then turn and face the mirror.

Zoom in to a close-up of my new and improved bazongas.

And . . . *cut!* Maybe Alexa had the right idea, but she definitely had the wrong size. Making a good impression is one thing, but trying to look like a tiny brunette version of Pamela Anderson? Quite another. I jump up and down a couple of times just for fun before I remove my new boobs.

With one more look in the mirror, I pack up my purse with orientation essentials: cell phone, three varieties of lip gloss, two pristinely blank notebooks, and plenty of good pens to doodle with.

My first order of business at school: find a group to hang out with for the rest of my career at Mythic High. I know it sounds silly, but it's a preemptive strike. And I know not to get my hopes up. High school girls are not known for their warmhearted welcoming qualities. That's why my plan is to infiltrate the ranks of the C-list: that low-key, nondescript clique associated with a specific extracurricular activity that is neither worth envying nor making fun of. One perk of the C-list is that it's usually coed (see: band geeks, drama nerds, cross-country runners).

Satisfied, I give my hair a last flick of the brush, and I'm off to the kitchen.

At the breakfast table, my mother is telling my dad all about some article she read in the *Mythic Gazette* this morning about all these dead fish found on the beach. Apparently, all the crazy weather happenings are messing with the local ecosystems.

Another point for Mythic on the craposity meter. Even the local wildlife can't survive here.

Despite the obvious sadness of ecological damage, I am forced to notice that my parents are nauseatingly cheery this morning. I maintain my practiced "whatever" face lest they attempt to sucker me into their senseless merrymaking.

"Just think, Sophie," says Dad the delusional, "soon it'll be Halloween in the deep, spooky woods of Massachusetts! And judging from all the jack-o'-lanterns I saw on my jog this morning, I'm betting Mythic still goes all out—same as when I was a kid!"

"Yeah, I know, you've died and gone to heaven," I say, keeping my tone drier than a stale saltine. "But can we talk about the decoration thing? I mean, isn't there some sort of unwritten rule along the lines of, you know, no white shoes after Labor Day, no pumpkins . . . um, before it?"

"Oh, honey, I am so proud of you for jogging!" coos Mom. She ruffles Dad's hair, totally ignoring my grinch-who-stole-Halloween attitude. "We should all start taking morning jogs together. What do you think, Soph?"

I think I'd rather sip a venti mug of hot lead. I take another spoonful of cereal, which prevents me from having to respond.

For the next ten minutes I chew bran in silence as my parents excitedly talk about their first effort to raise money to save Mythic.

I swallow the flakes with difficulty. Is there really so much here that's *worth* saving?

Summer and Scott debate the merits of hosting a "fact-finding gathering," to which they will invite all the town bigwigs. But before they can do that, my mother interjects, they need to get the house in shape. This includes the purchase of gothic lawn ornaments for our new enormous yard or some such nonsense.

I roll my eyes. They're so pathetic, they're excited by the *lawn*. I feel a sliver of pity for them until I remember that they're the ones who have exiled me from any sort of happiness.

Oh, great. Now they're holding hands and smooching over their gourmet coffee. Yuuuuckkkkk. They are grosser than the picture in the paper of the dead fish on the beach. Geriatric displays of affection at the breakfast table: I may well be put off cereal for life.

Crispy, who has been sitting at my feet purring contentedly, also seems repulsed by the display. He hacks up a hair ball, missing my cutely attired feet by about two inches.

Already, a promising start to the day.

6

There are crows circling over the gargoyle-adorned, iron-spiked bell tower of my new school. Thirteen of them. I counted.

A dark cloud momentarily covers the sun, casting the entire school in eerie gloomy darkness. The bell chimes nine, and each deep gong reverberates in my stomach. I'm starting to regret forcing down that bran.

Somehow, when I rode my bike past Mythic High's wrought-iron gates yesterday, I was able to ignore the looming creepiness of its ancient brick building. It is possible that turning my head away and refusing to look at it helped in this respect. But now, approaching the imposing stone steps that lead up to the main entrance, I have no choice but to stare my new school square in its unattractive face. It is three stories of imposingly solid-looking dull red brick and giant stones. And then there's that bell tower, which looks like ideal hunchback real estate. A few broken windows pay testament to the recent storms, but otherwise the tower is unscathed, rising defiantly, pricking the sky.

The whole structure looks more like some sort of satanic cathedral than a high school.

The high school I would've gone to in LA looked like a mall. A nice mall, with a quad and a burbling fountain. It's probably better not to think about it.

"It used to be a church," says a voice behind me. I turn to see Linc standing behind me, looking even cuter than I remembered in a ripped band T-shirt and dark jeans.

"Hey," I say, surprised. Then I gesture to the building. "A church? Really?"

"Yeah. Everyone in Mythic knows that. And we also already know everything they're going to tell us at freshman orientation. So most of us skip it."

"How? I mean, where do you go?" I have to admit, I hadn't been particularly looking forward to being the new kid at a big assembly.

"Just follow me," Linc says, leading me through the heavy, wrought-iron front doors.

The halls of Mythic High are just as eerie and hollowly high-ceilinged as you'd expect, painted a chalky black and white. The floor tiles are the wan pastel green of an after-dinner mint. They seem to wind off in all directions, but Linc leads me through them with a certainty that makes me wonder if this is his first crack at freshman year.

As we speed past rows of yellow lockers, I'm noticing a definite dearth of designer denim, oversized purses, and boots of any nature. Instead, most everyone looks like a particularly uninspired window display at some suburban mall in the Valley. Polos and henleys abound. Eastpak backpacks predominate. Nondescript Nikes pad along the shiny floors of the hallway. My hefty hobo weighs heavily on my shoulder as it dawns on me that "understated" might have a completely different meaning in Massachusetts.

"This way," Linc says, pointing at a stairwell.

For the first time, I pause. Maybe I should go to orientation after all. I mean, I don't know this guy very well, and there's no telling where he's taking me. Call me paranoid, but I've seen enough horror movies (well, enough horror movie footage) to know that sneaking off alone with the mysterious bad boy is usually something the expendable third lead does.

So I stop walking. "Um, I really don't want to get in trouble."

Linc just smiles, in a way that makes me feel dumb for being suspicious. "Chill out—it's the first day of school. We'll just say we got lost or something." He pulls me through a side door in the stairwell out into a courtyard.

We sit on a stone bench under an oak tree and watch the Gap ad masses march past. After we exchange a couple of monosyllabic comments about how we can't believe the summer is over already and school is lame, Linc sits back, and I can't really think of anything more to say.

Well, sitting with him is still way better than sitting by myself or in orientation. I let my gaze drift around the courtyard. Beige,

beige, straightened hair, totally last season Elsa Peretti necklaces, blah blah blah.

Uh-oh, there's Paul Pudnowski. I watch as one of the jocks in a letterman jacket "accidentally" bumps into him, causing him to drop the pile of books he was holding.

Just as long-suffering Paul crouches down to pick up his stuff, another jock comes by and "accidentally" kicks a book a foot or two away.

Wow, every teen movie ever made is right: high school jocks really are complete dirtbags.

As I'm turning away from the sad Paul Pudnowski scene, my eye catches a slightly more brightly colored group of girls in the corner of the quad. They stand out like peacocks in a flock of chickens. I can't see them clearly from here (I'm too vain for glasses, too lazy for contacts), but I do make out an incredibly cute anchor-printed vintage carryall, a pair of high, possibly suede boots, and a sweet, apple-patterned LeSportsac backpack.

A fashion oasis! I'm tempted to ditch Linc and go dashing across the courtyard. . . .

But when I turn to say goodbye, Linc is smoking a thin brown cigarette that smells sort of like air freshener.

"What are you doing!" I yelp, all thoughts of coolness tossed aside for now. "Are you smoking? You're going to get in trouble!"

"Chill out—it's just a clove cigarette. And no one gets in trouble on the first day of school!" Linc says, giving me a wink.

"Oh no? What are you going to say if you get caught? That

you didn't know smoking was against the rules?" I stand and start gathering my stuff. It sucks to have to abandon the one socially viable person who's been remotely nice to me, but I'm not going to let Linc drag me down into a pit of smoking iniquity. Especially not with a *clove* cigarette. Everyone knows that those things are made out of fiberglass, rat poison, and shredded old Camus paperbacks. Nothing I'd want in my lungs.

Linc laughs lightly. "And here I thought that being from LA, you'd be more sophisticated," he says, grinning devilishly. "Hey, watch my stuff for a second, Sophie, I'm just going to say hi to my boy Tino over there—I'll be right back."

"Uh . . ." I say, but he's gone. I toy aimlessly with the pack of cloves he left on the bench, inching it away from me with a stick as I watch him disappear into the crowd.

And then I feel a tap on my shoulder.

I look up and see a tweedy matron straight out of tweedy matron central casting—iron-colored bun, cable-knit cardigan and all—hovering over me. One of those old-fashioned HELLO MY NAME IS name tags adorns the right side of her . . . um . . . bosom (there's really no other word). This tag reads MS. LERNER. The reason I'm miserable in Mythic instead of happy in California. And *she's* glowering.

I follow her gaze to Linc's open pack of cloves.

"May I ask what it is you think you're doing?" she says in a chillingly quiet tone.

"Wha—uh—wait. Those aren't mine!" I stutter.

Ms. Lerner raises one eyebrow.

"They belong to the guy who was just sitting here," I explain. I'm about to say Linc's name, but I don't want to narc on him on the first day. "I'm sorry. . . . I'm new here. . . . I—I don't know who he was. . . ."

She smirks at me, not buying it for a second.

"Wait!" shouts someone from behind Ms. Lerner. It's Paul Pudnowski, and he's running in our direction. From the looks of it, he hasn't been doing much running lately.

"They're mine," he puffs. "Don't blame Sophie."

Ms. Lerner squints suspiciously at Paul.

"Paul Pudnowski, you know better," she says. "Your possession of these"—she picks up the cigarettes as if they were covered in toxic sludge—"means that you will have to report to detention at the end of the day. Since this is a first offense, I'll keep it between us. But next time, I'll have to report it to the principal, who will undoubtedly call your parents."

"I understand, Ms. Lerner." Paul nods.

"For now, I suggest you both get to orientation." Lerner walks away, leaving me and Paul staring behind her.

"Thank you," I say to Paul. "I can't believe you took the blame for that."

"No problem," he says, shrugging, "I knew she'd go easy on me. Lerner seems nasty at first, but she's actually a total push-over. And I wouldn't want you to get in trouble your first day of school."

"Well, that was really cool of you. I owe you one."

Paul grins at me. "I'll hold you to that, Sophie Stone."

I wander the winding halls for approximately a million years—the map that I got with my schedule is all but useless—but finally I do manage to find room 203, my homeroom for the rest of the year. It's been at least five minutes since the last bell rang, meaning I'm officially late. I sneak through the door as subtly as possible and slink toward a seat in the back row.

"Sophie Stone!" exclaims a voice from the front of the room.

Ms. Lerner. Of course. *She's* my homeroom teacher! Man, whatever I did in a past life was really, really, really bad.

Every head swivels toward me, and a whispery chorus begins. It sounds kind of like this: "Isshe . . . shshshshshsh . . . Spooky Stone?" This is like a nightmare come to life! I look down and double-check that I'm wearing clothes, because usually in this dream I'm naked or wearing a chicken costume or nothing but latex body paint.

But no, I'm fully clothed, and I'm fully awake. This is my real life, and it's actually happening to me.

I tiptoe past Ms. Lerner, ducking my head and giving her an ingratiating guilty smile. "Lateness is not tolerated in this school," she says sternly. I slink toward the very last desk, eyes glued to the linoleum tile, pretending not to hear the whispers.

Thank goodness something happens to distract everyone then. Another latecomer—a tallish, gorgeous-ish black girl in a crisp white button-down shirt—slips through the door, but before Ms. Lerner can lecture her, she wordlessly presents an official-looking slip of paper. Ms. Lerner glances at it, gives a brusque nod of approval, and the girl sashays to her seat, smiling contentedly.

Hall passes on the first day of school, eh? That girl is someone worth making friends with. Assuming that I'll be able to make a friend, ever. She joins two other girls—a redhead and a tiny brunette—in the middle of the front row. Looking at their bags and outfits, I realize that they're the "fashion oasis" I'd spotted in the courtyard.

I'm trying to think of ways to introduce myself to them when I feel something hit me on the back of my head.

"Excuse me," I say, swiveling in my seat. But the girl behind me (who sports Swiss Miss braids) is busy talking to the metal-mouthed girl across the aisle, completely ignoring me. I turn back around, a little more self-conscious now, if that's possible, and stare intently at the card with my schedule printed on it.

I feel another tap on my head. This time, I ignore it and give my hair a little toss. Classic California girl move. Of course, the little balls of paper that fall out of my hair render the move not so classic.

I know that reading the folded-up notes would just be giving the jerk(s) who threw them what they want, but I can't resist. Also, there's still a tiny outside chance that my standout style and rebellious lateness have won me my first secret admirer. I'm trying to be optimistic, okay? Anyway, I lean over as subtly as I can and unfold one of the notes in my lap.

Your outfit is scarier than any of your dad's movies, it reads. Ouch. Okay, not a secret admirer.

I hear laughter burst out behind me and turn to see two boys, one with big ears, the other with bright red hair, laughing while looking pointedly at me. I give them my sternest tough look and turn back around. So much for being popular thanks to my dad's fame.

A few moments later, another covert air attack catches me stingingly on the exposed nape of my neck, right under my ponytail.

"Ouch!" I exclaim.

Just like she didn't when it would've actually come in handy, Ms. Lerner turns away from the board. The rage in her eyes conflicts momentarily with a twitch of her mouth that seems to indicate some kind of sadistic amusement. "Sophie Stone. Would you *please* stop disrupting my classroom?"

The entire class titters and then goes back to filling out the emergency contact forms in front of them. I stare down at the boxes I'm supposed to be checking, trying not to think about how embarrassing it would be if I just suddenly burst out crying.

But nothing lasts forever, not even the worst homeroom experience of one's entire life, and soon the bell is ringing to signal first period. Everyone gathers up their stuff, barely pretending to listen to Ms. Lerner wrap her lecture about our new high-school-level responsibilities.

". . . and just one more thing before you all leave. Miss Stone, can you please stand up and come to the front of the room?"

At this point, it's clear that Ms. Lerner and I are having what my mom would call a "personality conflict." The conflict being that Ms. Lerner's personality is that of an evil shrew who probably keeps her underpants cataloged by the Dewey decimal system. And mine, obviously, is the personality of someone who is not okay with that.

"We have rules and regulations here at Mythic High that you may as yet be unfamiliar with, especially if you are new to the Mythic Township school system," Ms. Lerner lectures dramatically. "Can anyone tell me what rule Ms. Stone is violating?"

Great, I've somehow found a way to get into even *more* trouble. What did I do? Breathe the wrong air or something?

No one ventures an opinion, but from the way they're all looking at me, I can tell that I've already been found guilty by a jury of my peers.

Ms. Lerner grabs a thick volume off her desk. "*Mythic High School Rules and Regulations*, chapter 3, section C, part 26. 'Sartorial Recommendations.' 'Skirt length is to exceed fourteen inches or be no more than two inches above the top of the kneecap.'" She slams the book shut, that same sadistic smile playing across her pastily lipsticked lips. "I'm afraid, Sophie, that you're going to have to wear the blue raincoat today."

Can I just say, *Whoa*? Have my parents accidentally enrolled me in Holy Virgin Time Warp Christian Academy for the Extremely Prudish? I have to wear a blue raincoat to protect onlookers' eyes from an extra inch or two of thigh? I try to sputter something along these lines, but having twenty sets of eyes staring at you has a profound mouth-drying effect. I gape mutely as Ms. Lerner advances toward me, holding what appears to be the blue raincoat of shame: a mildewy-smelling sheet of aging plastic that looks like it was around to conceal unclad ankles back in 1910, which is probably when Ms. Lerner started teaching here.

As Ms. Lerner drapes the horrible coat over my shoulders (which have now contracted to about ear level), somebody finally speaks. The voice comes from the corner desk of the front row, and I have to swivel my head to see who it is.

"Ms. Lerner, will you please measure Sophie's skirt? Just so we're all clear about what is and isn't appropriate."

It's the hall pass girl. I'm too confused to know whether to glare at her or not, especially since there was a hint of challenge in her voice.

"Well, Devon, I suppose you're right," Ms. Lerner says. I try to make eye contact with this Devon—to see whether her motives are noble or sadistic—but her gaze is fixed on my hemline.

As Lerner fishes in her desk drawer for a ruler, I glance down at my skirt, trying to remember how big an inch is.

And then, so slowly that I'm sure no one but me can notice it happening, I feel my skirt . . . descend. I don't mean that it falls off or that it slides down from the waist. I mean that I feel the strings at its denim edge lightly brushing my legs as the skirt . . .

Okay, there's no other word for it . . .

It grows. My skirt grows.

Ms. Lerner leans down to make sure, then looks up from her ruler with a quizzical expression. "I could've sworn . . ." I hear her murmur under her breath. But then she switches gears, trying as hard as she can to look bored and indifferent to this unexpected outcome. As the second bell rings, she presses the humongous book she's just been reading aloud from into my hands.

"Miss Stone, you have narrowly escaped an infraction, by what cannot be more than a centimeter of fabric. Because you are a new student, I'll allow you to get away with it this time. But for the future, you will find a detailed description of Mythic High's dress code, as well as a vast amount of other information that you will no doubt find invaluable, in the Mythic High student handbook."

I stagger a bit under the leaden volume. The thing must weigh twenty pounds. It's like carrying a freaking Chihuahua and a half.

"You will read the first hundred pages and present me with a brief synopsis next week, Miss Stone," Ms. Lerner says. "Five pages should suffice."

That's brief? I give her a pleading look, but she only responds with a stiff nod. "Now, you'd better hurry on to your first class. You don't want to be late a second time."

Orientation day means short classes, so I'm back home in time for lunch. It's a good thing. After a first day like mine, there's no way I'm prepared to do the walk of shame through the cafeteria, searching for an empty seat in a room full of people who already know each other. That's tomorrow's torture. *So* much to look forward to!

I bellow a hello to my parents, clamber up to my room, and drag the Mythic High rule book out from my bag.

Homework on the first day. Total, total bummer.

I drop the book onto my bed, where it lands with a heavy thud.

I'm about to open the cover when I hear my bedroom door creak open.

"Mom?" I call out. But no one's there.

I could have sworn I shut my door tightly behind me.

An especially heavy cloud passes over our backyard, casting shadows and darkening my room. The silence in the house is so deafening, I can almost hear the drip-drip of the leaky faucet in the guest bathroom—two floors down.

A dark figure looms in the doorway. Wacky as my parents are, they are not the types to lurk outside my bedroom.

Before I can jump off my bed and slam the door closed to protect myself from whatever creepy crawly is out there, the door creaks open a few inches wider and in sashays Crispy. He stops just inside the room and stares at me, giving me a questioning "Meow?"

"Hey, furball," I say, relief washing over me. Crispy takes that as a welcome and proceeds to hop onto my bed. He settles down next to me and just stares, his amber-green eyes as blank as ever.

"You nearly scared the pants off me," I say, absently scratching between his ears.

Okay. Time to get this over with. I center the book on the comforter in front of me and open the cover. I flip past thick paisley endpapers to the first page of the book, which is blank. The next page should be the title page, and—

Huh, that's funny. It's blank too.

I flip a couple more pages. Blank, blank, blank. I open the book to the middle.

Blank.

A chill crawls up my spine. "What the hell is going on here?" I murmur.

And then, as I stare at the page, one printed sentence appears in the middle of it.

Welcome to Mythic, Sophie Stone

I slam the book shut. No. Freaking. Way.

Shaking all over, I pick the book up and try to open it again— just to confirm what I think I've seen—but I can't. My hands are trembling too hard. My head suddenly begins to throb, migraine-style. What is going *on* with me?

I can't, I think. *I can't deal with this, because you can only deal with things that are actually happening, and* this can't be happening.

But it is. Unless I'm going insane, the fact is, crazy things are going on with me. I have to accept that I'm holding in my sweat-soaked hands a book that, despite appearing to be a couple of decades old, somehow knows my name.

I close my eyes, breathe, and steel myself for another look at the page, but there's a knock at my bedroom door.

Dad pokes his head in—thankfully, he's not wearing one of his monster masks or the Grim Reaper's cape. "Hey, Soph!"

"H-hi, Dad." I gulp, wondering if he'll be able to tell that I'm the most freaked I've ever been in my life.

"I'm headed into town—your mom needs more tahini for dinner. Do you want anything?" He grins hugely and tousles my hair like I'm a four-year-old.

That's my father—*so* perceptive.

"No, but . . . Dad? Can I ask you something?" I say, my voice quivering.

His eyes light up. This is exactly the kind of cheesy parental-bonding moment he lives for. "Of course, Soph! You know I'm here for you when you need me. Ask away!"

I hand over the rule book. "Just open this for me and tell me if you notice anything . . . odd about it."

He does as he's told. I watch a puzzled expression play across his face. "Well, this is strange, all right."

"It is? You mean, it's not just me!"

He shakes his head. "No. Actually, I can't *believe* what I'm see-ing here."

I close my eyes in a silent prayer of relief. "So, what do we do about it?" I ask tremulously.

Dad shrugs. "I'm not sure, but you're going to have to scrap half your wardrobe!"

I frown. "What?"

"I mean, these rules are completely archaic. 'Girls must wear shirts that cover their collarbones'? Ridiculous! And I definitely don't remember it being this bad back in my day. In fact, *quite* the opposite."

Um, ew.

"Do you want me to call the school and complain?" Dad asks.

I stare at him wordlessly before grabbing the book back from his hands.

I expect to see the words he was just reading, but no. The entire volume is still blank to me.

"Soph . . . is something really wrong?"

"No, Dad." I take my eyes off the book. "It's just . . ."

It's *me*! I want to shout. There's something incredibly wrong with *me*.

But I can't tell him what's happening. He and Mom would commit me—or worse, use me to inspire their next screenplay.

"It's just . . . hard to adjust," I cover. "Things are different here, you know?"

Dad leans in and kisses the top of my head. "Don't worry, Sophie. You'll find your way."

I give him a halfhearted smile as he leaves the room, closing the door behind him.

The moment the door clicks shut, I crack open the book, flipping again though the blank pages. "What is going *on*?" I say in frustration.

Ink swirls on the page before me. Oh God, it's happening again!

A single word forms on the page.

Magic.

I drop the book and stare at it for a few seconds, my stomach in knots.

What is *that*? Was the book—was it *answering me*?

I shake my head.

No. Sorry. This is more than I can handle.

I kick the book off my bed, and it lands on the floor with a thunk. Crispy cranes his neck, startled by the noise. He jumps onto my lap, and I hug him tightly.

"Magic isn't real," I tell him, stroking his jet black fur.

Saying it out loud makes me feel a little better.

Maybe if I say it enough, it will start feeling true.

7

The following day I am striding down the halls of Mythic High. Ms. Lerner's book has been banished to a place beneath my bed. And the episode accompanying it? Buried just as deep. I have decided simply not to deal.

Denial, as a coping mechanism, is highly underrated.

I'm trying to avoid eye contact with any of the whispering masses, so I stare straight down as I walk the hallway. I'm nearly to class when the girl walking a few paces ahead of me drops her printed schedule.

"Hey!" I shout to her receding back. "You dropped this!"

No response. I check the name on the schedule, but like all our schedules, it only has the first four letters: ESME.

I give the girl, or at least the back of her, the once-over.

Raven hair—check. Backpack with safety-pinned patches for bands with names like Chalice of Malice and Satan's Toothbrush—double-check.

It's Esmeralda—the nasty witch from the Gift Shoppe, today playing the role of Mythic High's token goth girl.

Maybe I can use this twist of fate as an opportunity to get on her good side—after all, one less enemy can't but be a good thing.

"Esme! Hey, Esme!" I call.

Some of the kids walking alongside me stop cold. Esme turns around and locks eyes as if she's actually trying to melt my brain with her cold stare.

"Cursed nickname!" she growls.

Huh? What'd I say?

Her pierced lower lip and eyebrows are furrowed in rage. "Don't call me that!" she yells, nostrils flaring. Which, I must say, is not a good look for her.

"What? You mean, 'Esme'?"

"Lezzie Esme!" a boy shouts from behind me.

Even behind her pale powder, I can see Esme's face turn purple.

Ah. So Esme is not only the token goth, she's also the girl with the embarrassing nickname. A few of the rubberneckers start to snicker, and one gives an outright guffaw.

"It's *Esmeralda!*" she shrieks to the crowd. "And though I worship the goddess, I do not happen to be attracted to members of my own gender!"

She snatches her schedule from my hand. "Thanks," she snaps. "I *thought* I'd left those rumors behind in junior high!"

She turns and, with an overdramatic flourish, stalks away.

I sigh. It's official: Esme is my enemy. I will probably be turned into a toad before lunch.

I glance down at my schedule. All this drama, and I haven't even gotten to first period yet!

Geometry. Great. Is it possible to slit your wrists with a protractor?

"Hey, are you headed to geometry with White?" someone calls from behind me.

I turn, so overjoyed that anyone's talking to me at all that I almost forget to be disappointed when I discover that it's Paul Pudnowski.

Today, Paul is sporting a red T-shirt with white letters reading, DELA-WHERE? and brown corduroy pants that bag out at the knees. In another lifetime, I'd have been embarrassed to be seen with him. Right now, he's the only person I can remotely call friendlike.

Also, Paul is nice. I never realized how underrated niceness is.

"Here, let me see your schedule, Sophie Stone," he says, walking up alongside me. I hand the printout to him.

He scrutinizes the schedule for a second, then lets out a low whistle. "Whoa. They sure aren't going easy on you!"

"What do you mean?" I ask.

"Mrs. Ball for language? She's a tough one. And Mrs. White? My sister and her friends used to call her the Enforcer. She's a robot made out of steel and blackboard chalk." Paul is quite quippy, I'm noticing.

"Hmm, thanks for the heads-up."

"No problem. And hey, don't worry. We have geometry

together. I'll protect you from the Enforcer with my magical letting-you-copy-my-homework powers if necessary."

I smile at Paul, genuinely grateful. "Those powers might come in handy."

Once we get to the classroom, he sits at the desk right behind the one I pick.

Mrs. White isn't nearly as bad as Paul makes her out to be, but about halfway though the class, it begins to dawn on me that besides the social torment, I've completely forgotten the *other* aspect of school: the actual academic part. The part that in movies, they only show in montages—where people actually listen to lectures and take notes and get called on. *Eugh.*

I try to distract myself by doodling compulsively in my notebook.

Paul leans over my shoulder, takes in my sketch of the Enforcer. "Nice work, Sophie Stone. Good eye for detail. Think you can draw me one day? I'd like to look as tough as Mrs. White."

I snicker, then glance at Paul out of the corner of my eye. He leans back in his seat, satisfied.

Well, this morning hasn't gone too badly. Maybe the afternoon will be better. That is, if I can survive lunch.

Standing in line at the salad bar station, I covertly scope out the lunchroom landscape, hoping to pre-navigate a path to the closest deserted corner.

Thankfully, people seem to have stopped pointing and staring at me. I guess now that everyone has taken a peek at Spooky Stone's non-spooky offspring, they're already kind of over it. Which is fine by me.

Unfortunately, the cafeteria seems to be lacking any deserted corners. I'll have to actually sit next to (gulp) *people*. There's a table of jocks to my right—packed, of course, with meaty meatheads ready to carb-load before practice. Their cleats and shin guards are in piles alongside them, and they don't smell freshly laundered. Yeah, that table's out.

There's a group of skinny, vaguely burnout-ish kids at the next table over. I recognize one of the girls there from my history class.

Maybe I'd have a shot with her, I think. Then I notice that Ms. History Class seems to take undue relish in sniffing her Wite-Out.

Okay, maybe not that table either.

Eventually, I see a familiar face. It's Linc, joking around with the burnouts. He catches my eye and heads over.

"Well, well, well," I say. "If it isn't the Marlboro man."

"Hey," he says. "Sorry about what happened yesterday . . . By the time I realized you were getting in trouble with Lerner, Pudder had already shown up."

"That's okay." I decide on the spot.

"Come sit with me," he says, giving me an I'm-too-cute-to-stay-mad-at smile.

"Fine," I say coolly. Though inside, I'm thrilled beyond words.

Paul may have saved my reputation with the teachers, but Linc can save me from being a total loser.

I grab a cup of non-heinous-looking chicken noodle soup and head over to where Linc is sitting.

But before I can get there, I'm stopped short by the live-action American Girl doll herself, Corey Upton. She marches right up to me and taps me on the shoulder.

"Uh, hi," I greet her, and the two—what else is there to call them?—*minions* standing beside her. They're in triangular formation—like mini Charlie's Angels, but less fierce. There's a brunette and an Asian girl complementing Corey's blond. The three of them are sporting similar pink outfits and equally coiffed doll hair.

"I *saw* you flirting with my boyfriend just now," Cory snaps, "and if you think you can get away with stuff like that just because of who your dad is, you're so wrong."

I blink. Is she kidding? I mean, with this whole queen-bee persona? If so, I am not laughing.

"Uh . . . I wasn't flirting; he just asked me to sit with him because he knows I'm new here."

"Look, I don't care who you are—you just stay away from him. Got it?"

She punctuates this by putting her binder on a table and jabbing my shoulder with her finger. I'm startled and also clumsy. My shoulder jerks back and my tray clatters to the floor. But not before the contents of my soup bowl splatter unceremoniously all over Corey's—uh-oh—white angora sweater set.

Rivulets of chicken broth run down the front of her cardigan and spatter her khakis. Cory's expression? Picture a beached guppy gasping for air. It's kind of priceless. And hey: also kind of hilarious. So I can't help it. . . .

I laugh.

This does not make Corey or her minions happy.

"You idiot!" she screams. "What is funny about *this?*"

I decide not to explain, since her screaming has silenced the formerly buzzing cafeteria. I'm suddenly aware of hundreds of eyes on me. I compose myself as best I can.

"Ummm, I'm so sorry. Let me get you some napkins."

"Just go away," Corey spits as she turns, presumably to clean herself off. In spite of my misery, I get a kick out of the sight of little bits of noodle trailing in her wake.

I turn back toward Linc's table, and I'm surprised to see that he is nowhere in sight.

Oh, wait. Of course! I do seem to remember him beating a hasty retreat in the coffee shop when Corey showed up. I wonder momentarily about what's going on with her whole "my boyfriend" delusion when the object of her affection seems not to want anything to do with her. But for the moment, I have more pressing problems. Now lunchless and still seat- and friendless, I am at a loss. I'm turning to leave the cafeteria—perhaps to hide in a bathroom stall—when someone taps me on the shoulder.

"Hey," says a short, long-haired girl with a faint Euro accent. "Do you wanna come sit with me and my friends?" She smiles at me with unmistakable, genuine sweetness. She has a gorgeous, heart-shaped face framed by wavy light brown locks and a tiny body clad in a skirt, leggings, and a wraparound cashmere cardigan. Why she's being nice to me, I have no idea.

"Uh, sure, thank you," I say, falling into step behind her.

"I'm Cella," she turns back to say.

She leads me to a table where none other than Devon and the redhead from homeroom sit, and I quickly realize that without even having to do anything, I'm about to meet the stylish girls I'd dreamed of befriending yesterday.

Devon scoots her leather satchel over to make a spot for me next to them. There are a bunch of upperclassmen girls also at the table who nod hello, then quickly go back to their über-important conversations.

Devon, Cella, and the redhead are all looking at me, not unkindly, but not saying anything either. Clearly, it'll be up to me to make the first move.

"Hi, I'm Sophie Stone," I say.

"We know," Devon says. "How's that working out for you?" Her tone is playful, but there's compassion in her eyes.

I raise my hands in the universal "Isn't it obvious?" gesture. "I have to admit, I've had better days. I don't want to sound whiny or anti-Mythic, but . . . I'm miserable and I hate Mythic."

The girls look at each other and burst out laughing. "Well," says the redhead, "things can only get better from here. And I have a sneaking suspicion that you'll start to like Mythic sooner than you think." She reaches out her hand, gives me a firm handshake and an endearingly crooked smile. "I'm Katherine, by the way." I can't help but grin back.

"Hey, this might help make your life a little easier," Devon jumps in. "Next time you're late, just flash one of these." She presents me with one of the hall passes she handed to Ms. Lerner yesterday. It's embossed with the school seal, and if it's a forgery, Devon is a CIA-level operative.

"How did you get it?" I ask.

She winks at me. "I have my ways. Just make sure to use it soon."

"Yeah, they, um, expire," Cella explains.

There is a tiny moment in which my new lunchmates exchange glances. It's about to worry me, but the moment ends as abruptly as it began.

"Hey! Killer aim with the soup," says Katherine, toying with the pearls at her neck. Some people wouldn't pair real pearls with a faded Clash T-shirt, but on her it somehow works. She has one leg tucked up on her seat, and she's wearing a black cutout knee brace as though it were some new kind of accessory. Seriously, it looks great on her. "Corey deserved her soaking! I wish I'd thought of it."

"I don't know. I mean, I can't really endorse alienation of the ruling class," I say. "Makes for uncomfy strolls down the hallway between periods."

"Who, Corey?" Devon scoffs. "Please, she barely even rules her own hairdo. And anyone who would avoid you because of her isn't worth knowing anyway."

"Trust me, there are way more important things for you to worry about than Corey Upton," says Katherine.

"At least the soup didn't get on your boots. . . . They're so awesome," Cella adds quickly.

I blush at the compliment. It feels like the first nice thing anyone has said to me since I moved to this town.

"You seem to be the only one who likes them. I've been getting all kinds of weird looks."

"No one in Mythic has an understanding of fashion that goes deeper than J. Crew. It's tragic, really. But there are lots of interesting things about Mythic, in spite of its love of twinsets," Cella offers.

"Well, nothing against Mythic . . . I mean, no offense, this town *is* . . . interesting. . . ."

"You miss LA. And you must be a little bit freaked out, right?" Cella asks, and I nod. "Well, I can relate. I was born here, just like these two, but I was raised mostly in Spain. We moved back when I was ten, and I just hated everything about Mythic. I pretty much cried for a month straight and spent hours IMing with friends and never went outside."

"Not that that sounds familiar or anything." Cella smiles.

"Anyway, these two helped me a lot that first summer. They

taught me all the good English swear words, told me which boys were now cute, that kind of thing. And eventually I realized that it wasn't so bad, as long as we had each other."

Devon chimes in. "Boston's not too far away, you know. It's not as big a city as LA, but the shopping's pretty good. And most of the people in Mythic are harmless."

"Oh, really? Harmless?" I tilt my head in the direction of Corey and her posse. She's frantically swabbing at her stained sweater, and her minions are giving us dirty looks. "Corey What's-up-hers-ton seems positively evil."

"Oh my God. Corey. We *haaate* her," Cella says. "What she did to you is so her style—trying to hate and berate her way to the top of the social ladder. And she's been doing it since—"

"Since preschool. Literally," says Devon.

"But seriously, don't worry about her," says Katherine. "A girl who spends every night curling her hair with hot rollers is not worth being intimidated by."

"Hot rollers?" I ask, mock-horrified.

"Yup." Devon nods. "That's what it takes to get that doll-wig look she loves."

I picture Cory in bulky metal rollers. The mental image is priceless. "Can she be wearing one of those pore strips on her nose and fuzzy pink princess slippers too?" I say, and everyone cracks up. Things are definitely looking up.

Well, except for one thing: a certain curly-headed someone has just appeared beside our table. "Looks like you've figured out who's stupid enough to hang out with a spaz like you," she says in a gross, candy-coated tone of voice.

"Oh, lay off, Corey. We're not interested in your drama. In fact, you can . . ." Katherine starts, but Cella shushes her.

"Corey, Sophie didn't mean to spill her soup on you. How about giving her the benefit of the doubt?" It's noble of Cella to try, but it's also preposterously idealistic. Judging from what I've seen of Corey, Cella would probably have an easier time getting Lindsay Lohan and Hilary Duff to kiss and make up.

Except maybe it's working: Corey's smiling at Cella, and she looks like she's reaching out her hand to shake on a truce.

But then her hand moves to the side an extra inch . . . sending Cella's Coke skidding across the table, splattering all of us.

"Oops! My bad," simpers Corey. "Well, obviously *that* was a total accident. I'm sure you'll give *me* the benefit of the doubt too." She slinks off, her posse behind her, twitching her khaki-clad butt from side to side in a way that makes the tight ball of rage in my chest clench a little more tightly.

I look around at the other girls' faces—they all look just as angry as I feel, even peace-loving Cella, whose cashmere has borne the brunt of the cola damage.

"Welcome to Mythic, Sophie," says Devon. "You now have friends. But unfortunately, those friends have an enemy."

8

It's official: I've survived two weeks in Mythic. That's the good news.

The bad news? I still haven't handed in the stupid essay on the student handbook that Ms. Lerner assigned me on day one.

Eventually, Ms. Lerner is going to ask for her report. And the old "words just don't appear on the page unless I ask the book a question" excuse is probably not going to cut it.

Plus, in the sober light of day, I have to ask myself—is that what *really* happened?

I *had* just been through a very stressful move. And the angst of my first few days was nothing to sneeze at. Couldn't the whole crazy incident be explained by frayed nerves and an overactive imagination?

Perhaps.

I'm considering removing the volume from its hiding place beneath my bed and giving it another try when it dawns on me that the *thunk, thunk, thunk* I'm hearing isn't generated by my iPod. It's coming from outside—specifically, the window.

"Dad, you've done this scene already in *Night of the Harridan*," I shout, turning off the music. Pranks are so not about to go over well with me right now.

"What's that, honey?" I hear my dad call from his study. "I'm on the phone with the mayor. Did you need something?"

"Um, nothing," I call back. Huh. If my dad is inside, who on earth is *out*side? I shut off my lights and inch over to the window, then peek through the curtains, trying to be as covert as possible.

I recognize the prankster immediately. With a huff of irritation, I pop open the window—and a pebble whizzes straight into my forehead.

"Ouch! What the—"

"Whoa! Whoa, sorry, Sophie Stone! My rocks-at-the-window thing wasn't intended as an assault," Paul Pudnowski calls from three stories below.

I gaze down at Paul, who's staring up at me, smiling and squinting into the sun, shading his eyes goofily.

Huh. The sun. Haven't seen *that* in a while.

"Go away, Paul, I'm doing my homework," I call down to him.

"Crap, you totally hate me now," Paul says. "I should've gone for the pinecones instead. More aerodynamic, less dangerous."

I smile. Paul really is kinda funny. It's a shame he isn't more—understood by his peers.

"Well, remember that next time," I say.

"Next time?" Paul asks with a cheesy grin. "So, I'm invited back for an encore?"

I roll my eyes and start to back away from the window.

"Wait! Kidding! Completely kidding!" Paul says. I lean back out with my best patience-of-a-saint pose.

"What are you even doing here?" I ask. "Didn't anyone ever mention to you that it's not polite to lurk outside young ladies' windows?"

"Well, despite how it looks, I am really and truly not a stalker," he says, grinning so dorkily I kind of have to believe him. "I was just visiting my grandma, who lives a couple of houses down. I noticed your bike propped outside and realized you lived here."

"How'd you know which one was my room?" I ask.

"Lucky guess, and also that wind chime hanging on the balcony has your name on it."

I turn to look, and sure enough, there is a rainbow-colored wind chime, with my name spelled out on top, hanging from the railing.

I recognize this wind chime. Mom made it when I was five. It was an item I'd hoped we'd "forgotten" in LA. No such luck.

I stare down at Paul, who grins from below. I get the feeling he'd be willing to do this all day.

"Okay, well, I gotta go," I tell him. "Homework and all. Thanks for stopping by. . . ."

"Is it geometry homework? You know, that's my area of expertise." Paul points to himself. "Math whiz. It's a geek thing."

Tempting, but I feel like inviting Paul into my room might give him the wrong idea. It also might give my parents the wrong idea. The last thing I need right now is Dad sniffling over his little girl getting a "boyfriend." It would kill most of his fans to know it, but my dad is a total softie.

"Maybe tomorrow at school, Paul. Okay?"

He smiles, gracefully conceding defeat. "Okay. See you at school, Sophie S—"

"Paul." I cut him off. "Do you know another Sophie?" I ask.

"No, and I know what you're getting at. I just like alliteration. When you're a Paul Pudnowski, you sort of have to."

I can't help it. I smile again. "Okay, see you around, Paul Pudnowski."

"Ditto, Sophie Stone."

I watch him walk away, then shut the window. What a total weirdo. But in a way, kind of a cute weirdo. I try to imagine kissing him, but I catch myself recoiling.

No, I definitely don't like Paul that way. But thinking about kissing reminds me of someone else. As I return to my bed, I find myself imagining what it would be like to kiss Linc Montgomery. I feel a little twinge in the pit of my stomach. Mmm.

In spite of the fact that we haven't spoken since our awkward incident in the caf and in spite of his being taken—well, maybe not taken, but at least deemed off-limits by Corey "Crazypants" Upton—I guess I still have a bit of a crush on him.

Well, I'm sure I'll get over it. And what better way to distract myself than by writing a fascinating essay about Mythic High's rules and regulations?

I heft the tome out from under my bed, and my head suddenly begins to throb. Ignoring the pain, I open the book to the first page.

"So, where should I begin . . . ?" I mutter.

I feel a jerk and gasp as—there's no other way to describe it— as the book *leaps from my hands.*

It lands at the foot of my bed, where the pages begin to whirl, turning themselves in rapid succession, flying in a cascade of paper.

Finally, it comes to rest about midway through. Black ink swirls on the page's surface.

Begin at the beginning, the book says. *Find the coven.*

"No!" I yelp.

My head is pounding now. I shakily stand up, grab the book, and shove it into my bag.

I spend a moment regaining my breath.

I don't think I can go any longer without telling anyone about my headaches. The question is, who do I trust enough to tell?

When the answer comes to me, I realize that I kind of knew it all along.

9

Devon slams her palm down on the counter at Strange Brews.

"Garçon! A latte! I have a twenty-page essay to write in German tonight. And it's about metaphysics!" she announces—somehow in a non-obnoxious way.

"Okay, Ms. Graham," Paul jokes from behind the counter. "I'll make sure to sprinkle a little less crazy on it this time."

I crack up. What? It was funny. But I notice none of my friends are laughing.

In the daylight, I almost stop believing that what happened last night was real. And I definitely question why I'm on the verge of telling my new friends about it. Devon, Katherine, and Cella are so nice, so cool, and, most of all, so emphatically *normal*. If I mention that I've been seeing things, won't they try to have me put away?

I mean, the last thing I want to do is lose these girls' friendship. They're really turning out to be quite awesome—even in some ways that my friends back home weren't.

Devon is your classic overachiever. She's determined to take

as many credits as the Mythic school system will allow, so she is constantly staying after the final bell to study new economic models for Latvia and stuff.

Cella dances ballet and speaks fluent Spanish. And Katherine is a superstar athlete—soccer, field hockey, softball, and probably more—with a dry sense of humor.

Well, she'll need a sense of humor to deal with what I'm about to say.

"So, listen, guys. I wanted to talk to you about something that's been happening to me since I got here, but I'm worried that you'll think I'm a huge weirdo. Or a hypochondriac. Or maybe both."

The girls give each other significant looks. I'm starting to kind of hate moments like these—moments when it becomes clear that no matter how much these girls like me, I'll never be one of the original members of their clique. It's probably how the replacement member of Destiny's Child felt at first.

I try to ignore it while I launch into my story. The girls keep surprisingly calm while I'm speaking.

"I keep getting these strange headaches—like migraines or something. And I get them at weird times. Like when I try to open the school rule book that Ms. Lerner gave me on the first day. I know it doesn't make any sense, but I'm kind of thinking I might be, like, allergic to Mythic?"

Cue another awkward silence. I'm becoming the prime minister of Awkwardsilenceland.

I knew it. I knew I should have kept my mouth shut.

"Well, I don't think it's possible to be allergic to a town. But it seems like there might be more going on here. Like, when else do you get the headaches?" Devon asks.

"Uh, you know, just random times," I say. I'm so not going into this now. This was a mistake, and I need to reverse course. So I do what I always do when I get nervous: jabber on and on about total nothingness. "I know it's totally weird. All my life, all I've wanted is to be normal. Growing up with Spooky Stone as a dad was hard enough. It would be different if my dad was, like, Steven Spielberg or something. But Spooky Stone attracts kind of a different fan base. Since that first time a nasty kid in school started humming the theme song to *Zombie Nation* whenever he walked by me, I've always wished I could just be . . . you know, a regular person. And now this weirdness happens."

I say this last part quietly, to my lap. Man, I really need to learn how to shut it. Glancing up, I see that the girls are exchanging meaning-heavy looks . . . *again*. Finally, Devon speaks up.

"Normal is boring, Sophie. Why would you want to be boring?"

"I don't know." I shrug. "I guess because being anything else just causes problems."

Katherine grins and punches me on the arm like we've just lost a tough game of field hockey together. "No problems here, Soph. And don't worry about the headaches. Those will go away."

I smile gratefully at her. I'm still confused, though. I mean, how does *she* know they'll go away?

"So . . ." she says, looking deep into my eyes. "What's your favorite one?"

"My favorite what?"

"Your favorite Spooky Stone flick," she asks, maintaining intense eye contact.

With Katherine, I'm finding, there's always a right answer and a wrong answer—and you'd better answer correctly. Everything with her has a hint of challenge.

"Um. . . well, I'm not a huge fan of any of them, really. I've never seen a single one the whole way through. I do like some parts of *Deathscapade*," I hazard.

I catch a glimmer of disappointment from Katherine, but it quickly blows over. "My favorite one is *The Makings of Magic*," she says.

"Huh. The one about the witches? I always thought that one was a little cheesy. All that hocus-pocus." I shrug. Katherine gives me something that verges on being a dirty look. Call it a lightly soiled look. I have no idea what it's about.

"Here's your latte, Devon," Paul says, walking over with our orders. "We just ran out of caramel for the macchiato, so I made you a regular. Hope that's okay?"

Katherine assures him that it is. Paul puts my cappuccino in front of me, along with a raspberry scone.

"Oh, Paul, I didn't order a scone," I say.

He blushes, mumbles, "It's on the house," and walks away.

The girls give each other raised eyebrows. What now?

"Sophie, you didn't tell us you had a secret admirer," Cella whispers.

I wince. "You guys, Paul and I are just friends. He likes me because I'm nice to him. Seriously. It *is* possible to be friends with someone of the opposite sex." At least I hope so. . . . It's not like I have much experience with it myself.

"Yeah, well, you might want to be a little careful with him," Katherine says. "He can be a little intense."

"What do you mean?"

"She means he was hanging around the three of us all summer," Cella says. "We wondered why he stopped all of a sudden when school started . . . but I guess he just moved on . . . to *you*."

"Paul's kind of . . . weird," Devon puts in. "If I were you, I'd give him the brush-off."

Katherine nods in agreement. "The sooner, the better."

I have to say, I'm a little stunned. Sure, Paul's a geek, but I didn't think these girls would mind him hanging around.

I want to ask for more details—to find out why they feel this way—but just then a totally hot guy sidles up to our table. Dark brown hair, green eyes, letterman jacket—it's Jake Wallace, Katherine's boyfriend. He's a little too stereotypically jocky for me to take seriously.

"Hey, babe," he says, giving Katherine a kiss and stealing her coffee, which he swigs from deeply, like it's a post-game Gatorade.

"Mmm. Caramel macchiato."

"Don't drink it all," Katherine scolds, mock-annoyed.

"I thought Paul said he was out of caramel?" I ask, genuinely confused.

The girls shift around, looking uncomfortable. There are strange undercurrents here, but I can't tell what they're about.

Jake is completely oblivious.

"Well, I'd love to stay and hang out with you ladies, but I've got to study for my algebra test. If I want to stay on the soccer team, I have to pull at least a B." He leans in and chats with Katherine briefly, too quietly for me to hear over the din of the coffeehouse.

"I thought Paul gave you a regular coffee?" I ask again when Jake walks away.

"It is a regular coffee," says Katherine uncomfortably. "Jake was just kidding around. Inside joke."

I don't remember anyone laughing. I'm about to say something more about it when Devon leaps in. "Okay, girls, time to crack the books! Chop, chop!" she says in a dead-on impersonation of Ms. Lerner. "These essays aren't going to write themselves!"

Cella and I groan in unison. Nice to see I've got a comrade in homework-hating. "Too bad there isn't some spell to make homework do itself," I joke.

The girls look up, bug-eyed.

"What? I was kidding." The girls give nervous giggles and go back to their homework. I feel like I have to say something to diffuse the air of total weirdosity. I reach for my coffee and take a sip.

"Funny," I say. "*My* coffee tastes like caramel."

"Oh, sorry," Katherine says reflexively, and then looks embarrassed.

"What are *you* sorry for?"

"Um, our cups must have gotten switched?" This is blatantly not true, since my mug has a pale pink lipstick ring on it, clearly marking it as my own. What is going *on* here?

I glance over at Paul and find him wiping down the counter. I catch his eye, and he smiles, lifts his hand in a small wave.

I turn away before he has a chance to finish the gesture and make up my mind to ignore whatever weirdness is afoot, for the moment at least.

There's nothing to be gained by being curious. Go too far down that path and you'll end up like the girl who goes into the woodshed to try to figure out where that odd noise is coming from.

We all know where she ends up, and I'd rather be the girl who's still around for the sequel.

10

In hindsight, perhaps things were going a little too well for me.

I hadn't had another headache since my last run-in with the Mythic High rule book. I had actual friends, saving me from total reject status. And I even had a potential love interest in Linc Montgomery.

Farewell, run of not-so-bad luck. You were cool while you lasted.

It started out this morning, with a storm that the weatherman said was "stalled off the coast."

Translation: forget cats and dogs, it was raining saber-toothed tigers out there, closing streets and flooding basements. Getting to school took fifteen minutes longer than normal. And when you're me, those fifteen minutes are *crucial*.

I just about have time to tame my windblown hair and make it to homeroom. My butt is literally hovering above my seat when I hear a familiar voice call my name.

"Miss Stone," intones Ms. Lerner, before I can even sit, "you were assigned an essay on the first day of school. An essay you have yet to turn in."

"I—I can explain," I begin, wondering how on earth I am going to come up with an explanation.

Ms. Lerner raises her slightly unkempt eyebrows.

Corey Upchuckton chooses that moment to sashay to the front of the class and hand Ms. Lerner a sheaf of paper.

"Here, Ms. Lerner. It's that extra-credit essay you said you'd check over before I handed it in for Mr. Gorevitch's class. It's not due for another week, but I finished it early—thank you so much for offering to help me with it."

Lerner takes the papers with a nod, then turns back to me. "Miss Stone, you would be wise to be more like Miss Upton. You must hand in your report. I don't think you understand the importance of that book and what it contains."

Ugh. She's taking a dumb essay pretty seriously.

"I—I'm sorry," I stutter. "I'll get the essay to you next week."

Ms. Lerner gives me a pointed look. "Yes, you will, Sophie, or we will be discussing some very serious consequences."

As Ms. Lerner turns back to the board, Corey shoots me a smug grin, which enhances my shame a zillionfold. I sneer back at her, trying to hang on to a last shred of my dignity.

"Her parents were probably too busy teaching her how to whip up a realistic batch of fake blood," Corey hisses.

The rest of the classroom titters.

"I mean, what a freaky family," she continues. "Can you imagine having a person like that for your dad?"

I glance over at Ms. Lerner. Surely she won't approve of Corey talking out of turn. But she seems to have gone momentarily deaf.

I clench my fists. *Stupid Corey Upton,* I seethe. *She thinks she's so perfect. Her perfect hair, perfect makeup. Just once I'd like her to show everyone how nasty and rotten she is on the* inside.

There is a rumble outside, most likely from the storm.

And then it starts.

At first I think that there's another clap of thunder coming or that several people have pushed their chairs across the floor in unison. But the sound keeps rumbling—and a moment later, it doubles in volume. People are glancing around in every direction, trying to figure out where it's coming from.

And then, all at once, everyone discovers the source of the sound. It's about the same time that we notice the smell.

It's coming from Corey's khaki-skirted behind. That's right: perfect Corey Upton is having a fart attack that would put all the denizens of *South Park* and the entire cast of *Jackass* to shame.

It smells like a tractor-trailer carrying twenty tons of rotten eggs—after it's been rear-ended by a tanker carrying the dung of a thousand circus animals. And it just keeps going. Corey may be setting some kind of world record!

This clearly hasn't been a lifelong goal, however, because as the laughter and squeals of *"Gross!"* build to fever pitch, Corey makes a break for the door, sobbing uncontrollably. We can hear her continuing to fart as she sprints down the hallway, the steady *poooot poooot* growing more and more distant until it's just a small buzz.

Lerner tries to quiet down the chaos, but it's no use. This is clearly something that no one is going to shut up about for days—possibly years. Besides, decorum seems a little much to ask for in a room that, in spite of the windows hastily cracked open, still smells like an overturned Porta Potti that's been used by elephants.

"Class dismissed!" Lerner finally calls out, over the cacophony of hysterical laughter. It's only a minute or so till the bell, anyway. Everyone makes a mad dash for the door, and I am no exception.

For a second, I feel a bizarre pang of guilt. But that's insane. I didn't have anything to do with Corey's gastrointestinal assault. How could I have?

I absently rub my forehead, where the dull pain of a headache is throbbing.

The moment I open my eyes on Saturday morning, the first thing I think of is the book—and that stupid essay. But thankfully, I have no time for that today.

Today I will be busy being a normal teenager. Katherine's boyfriend, Jake, is on the Mythic High soccer team, and she invited me and Devon and Cella all to come and watch his first game.

My first high school sporting event! Wardrobe decisions need to be made. I've toned down my boots-and-layers-centric LA aesthetic in response to Mythic's staid prepposity, but today's perfect fall weather (not raining for a change!)—and my need to distract myself as much as possible from more-pressing issues—inspires me to put together a truly outstanding ensemble. At least, I think so. My purple Nikes show my school spirit (purple and black are Mythic's appropriately gloomy colors), and my skinny jeans and vintage coat show my style. As I ride my bike down the sun-dappled path that leads to the soccer field, I've almost managed to put yesterday's in-class weirdness out of my head completely. Uh, almost.

The bleachers are packed and loud with the voices of talky teenagers and bright with team colors. I'm not sure how I'll find my friends, but then I spot a gorgeous purple angora shrug and a long, light brown braid in front of me.

"Hey, Cella!" I shout.

"You made it!" She backtracks, grabs my arm, and we walk up the bleachers together to the topmost seats, where Devon and Katherine are already sitting. They both give big smiles when they see us approaching. I'm so happy to see them that for a moment, I toy with the idea of telling them that the Mythic school rule book knows my name. I know, it's a crazy idea. But I have to tell *someone*.

Maybe Paul would be a good confidant? Maybe. Except that my friends have put a kind of moratorium on hanging out with him. If what they said about his stalkerishness is true, then who can blame them? But I do feel kind of bad. Every time I walk by him in the hallway without saying hi, I feel his big, puppy dog eyes following me.

Besides, after you tell someone of the opposite sex your deepest, darkest secrets, you're usually obligated to make out with them afterward. I think the answer is just to suck it up and try to figure things out on my own.

I take a quick glance at everyone's outfits, just to be sure I fit in. Yup. Devon's in a sporty but glam set of perfect grayish jeans and a white blazer, and Katherine is wearing a hot teal-and-purple polo that opens to show a few cute freckles below her clavicle. She's also sporting a decidedly pissed-off expression, and it seems like we're all about to find out why.

"So check it out," she says, not even waiting till we take our seats. "You'll never believe the outrage I just witnessed. I was waiting by the locker room, you know, to wish Jake a good game, and guess who was already there, hanging all over him? Madison Wright! That skank."

"Really? She was flirting? I can't believe her," says Cella. "Was he, you know, reciprocating?"

"Isn't it enough that *she* was going after *him*?" Katherine non-answers. I get the sense that what she really means is, "Yes, but I'm too proud to admit that my boyfriend flirts with other girls."

"What were they doing exactly?" asks Devon.

"They were just talking. But she kept on rubbing his arm and complimenting him on how he looked in his soccer uniform. . . ."

We all groan.

"Freaking cheerditzes." Katherine spits the words." Vapid little—"

Cella cuts her off before we find out what she was going to call Madison and her pom-pommed cohorts next. "Look! The game is starting."

"Oh, are we really here to watch?" I ask, surprised. I'd assumed that the game was just a thinly veiled excuse to ogle guys and gossip. But the girls' eyes are immediately glued to the field below, where our team, in purple, is preparing to kick off against a group of boys in white jerseys.

"We're playing the White Knights from Salem High," Devon informs me. "They're our all-time rivals."

"What's that cone-shaped thing on the back of Mythic's team shirts supposed to be?"

"They're wizard hats," says Cella. "You know, for the Mythic Warlocks?"

"Our team is called the Warlocks?"

"Only the boys' teams."

"Do I even want to know what the girls' teams are called?"

Devon smirks. "We'll let you figure it out once you see them in uniform."

I'm picturing girls in long black robes and high-heeled mid-calf boots playing lacrosse when I see Linc. He's sitting to our right, a few bleachers down, and as I watch him laugh with his friends—a couple of guys who look a little older than freshmen—I get that fizzy feeling in my stomach again. Cella catches the direction of my gaze and says, "I heard they played an awesome show last weekend."

"Show?"

"Yeah, Linc and Tino and all of them. They're in this band called Crikey Moses. I've never heard them play, but we should go one night. It could be fun."

I'm about to respond when Katherine squeezes my arm.

"Oh my God, Jake's hurt!"

Cut to a shot of Jake, curled on the ground in the fetal position, clutching his calf with an expression of agony on his face. A collective gasp bursts from the crowd. The ref whistles, the crowd falls silent, and a coach runs out onto the field, with a little brunette cheerleader trotting close behind. Her too-short pleated miniskirt flaps wildly.

Madison Wright, I presume.

"What the hell does she think she's doing?" Katherine asks in horror. I'm with her one hundred percent.

Jake, meanwhile, seems to be recovering. He's stopped clutching his leg, and his expression is no longer quite so pained. But before he can lift himself off the ground, Madison kneels down by him and, taking advantage of his obviously vulnerable state, grabs his face *and kisses him.*

The crowd cheers. Katherine leaps to her feet, her eyes burning with rage. I'm seriously afraid that she's about to vault over the crowd's heads and onto the field.

The coach and another soccer player are now helping Jake to

his feet. They walk him off the field, sit him down on the bench, and hand him a Gatorade. Madison jogs back to her place with the cheerleaders. I catch her giving some ringleted blonde a high five.

Wait a minute. I recognize the blonde. It's Corey Upton. Of *course* she's a cheerleader. Why would I be surprised?

"That tramp is so dead!" Katherine says, her voice dripping with rage. Cella pats her hand reassuringly—ever the peace-maker.

"Chill, Kat. Don't sink to her level. There's nothing you can do."

I catch meaningful glance number one zillion passing between them.

Then the game takes a brief time-out, and the Mythic cheer-leaders begin an energetic cheer.

"GO! BANANAS! B-A-N-A-N-A-S! GO! B-A-N-A-N-A-S! You SHIFT to the left and you SHIFT! to the right, and you peel it down good and you, UNGH! Take a bite!"

I can't help but notice that this cheer doesn't have much to do with soccer. And neither do the dramatic video-ho hip thrusts that accompany each "SHIFT!" But then, asking cheerleaders not to dance like hos is pretty much like asking fish not to swim.

Oh, lame: people are beginning shouting along with the banana cheer. Madison is particularly obnoxious with her leg kicks and clapping.

"I can't stand it," says Katherine, who might as well be emit-ting steam from her ears at this point.

Out on the field, the chipper, shouting band of harpies has managed to arrange themselves into a medium-sized pyramid, with little Madison on the top. She rises to her feet atop another girl's back and does an impressive arm gesture as she and her cohorts continue to shout innuendo-laden things about fruit.

The wind, I notice, has picked up. But the sudden windstorm seems highly localized. That is, it's only in the cheer pyramid's general vicinity.

But . . . how is this possible? The girls' hair is whipping around as they valiantly attempt to stay in formation. It's hard to tell from here, but at least a few of them—the ones toward the top—are starting to look freaked out.

Our eyes are all focused on Madison as the gust of wind toys playfully with her itty-bitty skirt. And then, with one decidedly un-wind-like motion, the whole skirt flips up so that the hem is hovering somewhere around the top of the big *M* embroidered on her sweater.

I'd always thought that cheerleaders wore demure little boy-cut drawers under their skirts, but apparently Madison forgot hers. She's standing in front of the entire school in a leopard-print pair of what looks, unfortunately, like a thong.

Hoots and catcalls fill the stand.

As Madison tries to push down her skirt and regain her balance simultaneously, the wind continues to buffet the pyramid, which is looking more and more like a leaning tower of cheer.

It's a worrying sight—the top of the pyramid is pretty far off the ground. The hoots turn into worried mumblings.

For some reason, I choose that moment to pry my eyes from the action on the field and turn toward Katherine. Her rage-filled expression has changed—now her forehead is furrowed in concentration, like she's trying to figure out the world's hardest math problem.

"Stop it," Devon whispers urgently.

"Can't," whispers Katherine, her eyes still laser-focused on the field.

"Katherine, please," Cella begs. "This isn't funny anymore."

My mind whirls but can't quite process what's happening. I only know two things, and the knowledge seems to come from a place deep inside, nowhere near my conscious brain:

1. This (whatever "this" is) needs to stop before anyone gets hurt.

2. Somehow, *I* can make it stop.

I focus on the cheeramid. My head starts to throb.

Stop, I think, quiet as a whisper. Nothing happens, so I repeat the word in my head, each time a little louder, the pain in my brain a little stronger.

Stop. Stop. STOP. STOP!

And then I feel it happening. The wind dies down, turning into a mild breeze. The pain ebbs from my brain.

The cheeramid disassembles, and the cheerleaders retreat from the field.

Madison has her face in her hands—crying, I guess, either

from fear or embarrassment. The crowd snaps right back to normal as soon as the game resumes.

The girls and I, however, are sitting frozen in stony silence.

"Katherine!" says Cella. "I cannot believe you did that."

I glance over at Katherine, who looks like she may hurl. She's gone ghost pale; even her freckles look a little green. "I didn't mean to," she whispers. " My emotions got the best of me and I couldn't control myself. If you guys hadn't helped me out . . ."

"Uh, I tried to, but I'm pretty sure I didn't," says Cella.

"Ditto," says Devon.

In unison, the girls turn toward me.

For the first time since all this weirdness started happening, I am really, really scared.

"What just happened?" Devon asks, looking at me.

"You think *I* know?" I yelp. I feel like I'm about to start crying. The girls are now exchanging worried glances. Finally, Katherine breaks the silence. "I think we need to head someplace a little more private. Come on."

She leads the way down the bleachers and back toward the school. We're halfway down the field when a familiar voice stops us all dead in our tracks.

"Girls! Come here, please!"

We turn in unison to see a bizarrely attired Ms. Lerner walking briskly toward us. She is decked out in rah-rah chic: black Mythic High sweats and a Warlocks baseball cap.

Huh. Never pegged her as a sports fan. She's just full of surprises.

"Great," whispers Devon beside me. "What is *she* going to come down on us for?"

"Girls . . ." Ms. Lerner repeats with what looks like—can it be?—worry on her face. "All four of you are to report to my office immediately. There are . . . things . . . that must be . . . discussed."

"Things?" parrots Devon. "What kind of things?"

"That information will have to wait until we can discuss it in private," says Ms. Lerner, giving a subtle glance to each side. "We will all reconvene in my office in ten minutes. Don't be late." With this, she turns on her heel.

"Oh my God, do you think she *knows*?" whispers Cella, wide-eyed.

"*Knows*? I don't even *know*. What just happened out there?" I ask.

The girls exchange glances again, and I watch as they nonverbally elect Devon as their spokeswoman. "We don't really know anything—just that all of us, since the beginning of summer, have been able to do weird things. Usually by accident."

"Like toppling a pyramid of cheerleaders?" I say.

"That was an accident!" Katherine exclaims. Then she clamps a hand over her mouth.

Devon simply nods. "Yeah, and that's as much as we know. Oh—and we all just had this feeling, nothing we could explain, that you might be the same way."

I stare at my new friends and realize I don't know them at all. I don't even know *me* at all anymore.

"We should probably just head for Ms. Lerner's classroom," I mutter lamely. The girls accept my cop-out wordlessly, and we head in the direction of Mythic High's gothic-arched entrance-way. It looks even more foreboding than usual in the dimming twilight. I have no idea what's awaiting us inside, but I keep walking.

11

Ms. Lerner walks into her classroom to find us all perched on the edges of our seats, silently awaiting her arrival. We're all vibrating with nervous energy, and Ms. Lerner doesn't seem to be faring much better. She's clutching a coffee mug, taking small, businesslike sips. The mug shimmies in her hand a little, and I wouldn't bet on its actually containing coffee. She takes another wincing tug on her beverage and then, finally, speaks.

"I didn't want to have to intervene in . . . the natural course of things," Ms. Lerner begins. "But from the looks of what just happened, it seems I may have to."

"The natural course of things?" asks Devon.

"Your powers," Ms. Lerner says simply, cupping her mug with both hands and pointedly looking at each of us in turn. "Yes, girls. I know all about your powers," Ms. Lerner says matter-of-factly. "I know that they began on the summer equinox, as prophesied. How do I know? My dear friend Sophie

Mulvane—Sophie's great-aunt—was a witch in the last coven. A seer. And she left me the book to help guide you."

"What book?" Katherine yelps. "What are you talking about?"

Ms. Lerner *tsks*. "Now, girls, you all know the legend. A coven of witches is born to this town every other generation. This generation you, my dears, are that coven."

My head swims at Ms. Lerner's words. What is she telling us? The ridiculous fairy tale my dad told the day we arrived in Mythic . . . is *true*?

"I thought that was just a story," Cella says, reading my mind.

"I'm afraid it's not," Ms. Lerner continues. "You girls are each descended from the first coven of Mythic—women who inherited great power from the founders of the town. It took some doing to get you all here at precisely the right moment"—she nods in my direction—"but you *are* here, and now you must continue to pursue your destiny."

She turns to fully face me. "Sophie, did you read the book, as I asked you to?"

"Uh, yes," I squeak.

"And . . . ?"

There's another uncomfortable pause. A long one. Eventually, I give up hoping that everyone will forget Ms. Lerner was talking to me and move on.

"The book . . . well, it knew my name," I admit quietly. "It . . . it was like it was talking to me."

The girls give a collective gasp behind me and begin to talk all at once.

"Quiet, girls!" Ms. Lerner scolds. She waits a moment before continuing in her class lecture voice. "I was entrusted with the secrets of the last Mythic coven for . . . various reasons. One reason was my close friendship with Sophie Mulvane.

"Sophie, your great-aunt knew that you would need guidance when you came into your powers, so she gave you something she never had: a magical tool, to help you understand."

"You have no proof," Katherine blurts. "You don't know that we're . . . you know . . . the ones."

Ms. Lerner pauses, then walks back to her tote bag and pulls out what look like small pieces of loose leaf that have been jaggedly ripped to form small squares.

"Your hall passes," she says. "You four have been using them since school began. Did you really think that I wouldn't notice when they reverted to their non-magical state?"

Katherine and Devon both gaze at their desks guiltily. Ms. Lerner's face takes on a softer expression.

"Now, now. Don't be upset." She pats Katherine's hand consolingly. "You have been given a great gift."

"A gift?" I say, incredulous. "Katherine nearly killed someone with *her* gift."

"I didn't mean to . . ." Katherine says. Devon shushes her, as if admitting to the wind episode is the worst of what's going on right now.

I think of another "wind" episode—one involving Corey Suckton—and my cheeks burn with embarrassment. Maybe I'm not so different from Katherine.

"After today's display, girls, it's clear to me that your powers are not yet fully formed. It's for this reason that some of your magic does not have the desired effect." Ms. Lerner leans in, her expression grave. "Using your magic right now is like operating dangerous machinery without reading the instructions or hopping in a car and driving without ever having had a lesson. While it might be possible to get some things right, you might end up doing something more extreme than you'd wanted or doing the opposite of what you'd intended. And as we've seen today, that can be very dangerous."

Ms. Lerner stands. She is in full lecture mode now. I wonder if she's about to diagram something on the blackboard.

"Your powers will be at their strongest once you accept them and bind yourselves together as a coven. Ideally, this ceremony should be performed at Samhain, or Halloween. Sophie's book," she says, nodding at me, "will guide you. And"—she sighs—"I will attempt to help when I can. But Sophie is your greatest resource. She has the book, and, if the prophecy is correct, she will have the strongest powers."

An uncomfortable tension fills the room when Ms. Lerner says this.

I don't want the strongest powers! I want to scream. *I don't want any powers!* Ms. Lerner drains the final sip from her coffee mug, picks up her bag, and makes for the door.

She grasps the knob, then glances back. "I know you girls didn't ask for this power. But it is yours," she says. "You can do great things with it, and soon, you will have to do just that. I wish you luck." And with that, she exits. The door closes with a quiet click.

"This is crazy," I say to no one in particular.

"We need to see that book," Katherine says, still looking a little scared about what happened out on the soccer field.

"Are you nuts? I want nothing to do with this *witch* business," I tell them. "I'm from LA, for crying out loud! We don't *do* Wicca."

"Remember those headaches you were getting?" says Devon. "We all got them too. At first."

"Yeah," says Katherine. "They started whenever one of us would do magic, even if we didn't mean to. Which was like one hundred percent of the time at first."

"Then, once we started doing magic on purpose, the headaches slowly went away," says Devon.

"Well, I want all of this to go away," I exclaim. "This is just *not me!*"

Cella smiles sadly. "Sorry, Sophie, but I don't think this is optional. Like it or not, being a witch is part of who you are. It's like if I asked you to stop being a girl or to stop being from California."

Devon sighs in exasperation. "You heard what Ms. Lerner said, Sophie. We need accept our powers and harness them in order to be safe. And we need your help to do that. I know this is unbelievable and weird and not exactly the image you'd like to cultivate, but it's a part of you—a part of all of us."

"Well," I say, finally losing my temper, "I'm getting that part *removed*!"

12

I think I can say, with a certain degree of confidence, that high school is just some institutional social experiment, designed to test teenagers' responses to torture.

I mean, besides the inexplicable insanity of last week, which I still haven't even begun to wrap my mind around, there's also the endless torment of *education*.

Case in point: biology.

Today, Mr. Krueger, he of red felt bow tie and argyle sweater vest fame, informed us joyously that we will be dissecting frogs. I can't think of anything more disgusting and useless. I mean, at what point in my adult life will I need to know the inner workings of an amphibian? Answer: none.

My lab partner happens to be Paul Pudnowski, and *he* couldn't be more excited. He's been wearing his biology goggles all morning in glee. Which tells you a lot about Paul.

Cella, on the other hand, does not seem happy. She sits two

rows in front of me, and she is being very outspoken about her disapproval of this lab exercise.

The thing is, I haven't quite been able to, you know, *speak* to my friends since Saturday's trauma. So I don't know if Cella's been planning to protest or if it's something that occurred to her on the spur of the moment, and I turn around like everyone else as she stands up and starts yelling at the teacher.

"Mr. Krueger, I don't think we should all be required to participate in a lesson plan that involves animal abuse," she says, very righteous and indignant.

"Miss DeLeone, please sit down," says Mr. K. "This is a standard part of any high school biology course. There is no animal abuse involved. These frogs are already dead." He walks over to the supply cabinet, then adds for good measure, "Of natural causes, I'm sure."

"Oh, give us a break, Mr. Krueger!" Katherine chimes in. "Those frogs died because a pharmaceutical supply company raised them to die."

"Thanks, Kat," says Cella. "I refuse to participate, Mr. Krueger, on ethical grounds." She scans the room coolly. "I encourage everyone here to join me."

"Wow, Cella's really serious about this stuff," I whisper to Paul. I wonder if she has any issues about wearing furs or leather. I hope not—a scruple like that can really cramp a girl's style. Just look at Alicia Silverstone.

"You are free to sit in the principal's office for the remainder of the class, Miss DeLeone. But you will have to take a zero for the day."

"Another to add to her collection," Corey Upton murmurs before speaking up. "I don't find anything at all wrong with this exercise, Mr. Krueger. Dissecting and studying animals is an important part of scientific research. It's how we progress as a society, not only in understanding biology, but in medical advances."

"Point taken, Miss Upton," says Mr. Krueger.

"Corey, I think there's something on your nose," I whisper under my breath.

Paul, on cue, makes a gagging gesture, and I giggle.

I have to hand it to the guy. He didn't say a word about my recent bout of blowing him off when I latched onto him Monday morning.

He just carried on making wisecracks, happy as a clam. Or in this case, happy as a dork in safety goggles.

Which, all things considered, is pretty nice of him.

"I don't see how it's fair to give me a zero for not participating in a lab experiment that is against my beliefs," Cella argues. When this gets no reaction, she continues. "I'm not the only one in class who thinks this lesson plan is wrong."

"I don't see anyone else protesting, Miss DeLeone," Mr. Krueger responds.

"Katherine and Devon feel the same way," Cella says. I steal a glance at Devon and catch her rolling her eyes. I bet the idea of

taking a zero for the day isn't sitting well with Ms. Future Vale-
dictorian. But still, she and Katherine walk toward the front of
the classroom to stand with Cella.

Huh. They may be delusional about this witch stuff, but
they're loyal, for whatever that's worth.

"That is still a minority of students, Ms. DeLeone."

Cella now turns to the class. "A zero for the day is not going
to scare us. Anyone who's with me, raise your hand."

No one does. Corey snickers, then makes a big show of
politely muffling herself. Oh, man. I'm tempted to stand just to
prove her wrong.

"Guys? Come on! Danielle, Elena," she says, addressing the
two preps in the front, "do you really want to see frog guts right
before lunch?"

"Sorry, Cella," Danielle says. "If I get a zero in a lab, I'll get
kicked off debate team."

"Me too," Elena says, twirling her curly brown hair. "I can't
risk it."

Beside me, Paul is getting frustrated. "Let's just get on with
this!" he whispers. "I was born to dissect a frog! I've been dying to
know what's inside a frog since I was a little kid."

I grimace. "You are *so* weird."

I glance up again at the front of the room. Katherine, Devon,
and Cella are standing there together—a human chain of protest.
I glance over at Paul and see him twitch in anticipation of the
dissection he's been promised.

So here's the thing. I don't want to be a witch, but Paul Pudnowski is just not someone I can see identifying with my love of accessories. The ladies in the front? They're the only friends I've got.

And also: I really, really don't want to dissect a frog. Especially, as Cella points out, before lunch.

"I'll protest with you," I announce, standing at my seat.

"Sophie? What are you doing?" Paul asks in confusion.

"Sorry, it's a girl thing," I whisper before abandoning Paul and walking to the front of the classroom. Katherine smiles as I take her hand, joining the chain.

"You'll have to take a zero as well, Miss Stone," says Mr. Krueger, opening the supply cabinet. "And now, if you all are done with your little demonstration, please, the rest of us are going to dissect these frogs!"

"I still object to the fact that this is a required activity, Mr. Krueger!" Cella yells. It seems like she's completely lost her patience. I feel a strange energy running through me—like a small electric shock.

"These frogs should be alive right now, not floating in formaldehyde!" Cella continues. "They should be hopping around as nature intend—"

The sound of shattering glass cuts her off.

I scream as smelly liquid spills out of the cabinet, threatening to stain my . . . oh, crap, my velvet Balmain flats! I scream louder. And then, louder still, because along with the reeking formaldehyde, what's pouring out of the closet is . . .

Frogs. A biblical-plague-style wall of bright green *frogs*. And they're hopping right toward us!

Pure reflex propels me halfway across the classroom, which has erupted into chaos. Students are standing on their chairs, staring wide-eyed at the runaway amphibians. Paul actually scrambles atop the lab *table*, curling himself into a protective ball and shrieking like a girl.

I'm frozen in my tracks, mesmerized by the sight of the bright green creatures leaping around the room.

Wait—*leaping*?

"I thought these frogs were supposed to be dead!" Katherine yells above the din.

I lean in for a closer inspection as one little froggie flops arrhythmically down in front of me.

How do I put this?—there's something sort of stiff about these little guys. Their eyes look unusually red and bugged out. And they're not acting normal. As I watch, the frog in question hops right past me and straight into the wall with a loud *smack*. He gets up and does it again, and again, and again—like a windup toy.

I shake my head. I can't believe it.

Welcome to *Afternoon of the Living Amphibidead.*

And say hello to the zombie frogs.

I grab Devon's arm to tell her there's a frog on her Puma and feel that strange tingling in my fingers again.

"What's going *on*! Who *did* this?" wails Elena as she kicks uselessly at the frog onslaught.

I suspect—no, wait, I know—the answer to her question.

I glance at Devon, then Cella and Katherine, and see that they're thinking the exact same thing. What just two days ago I would have dismissed as an annoying prank now troublingly feels like my fault.

Or, more precisely, *our* fault.

"Now do you see why we have to figure out how to use our powers?" Devon asks.

I close my eyes and nod silently.

Oh my God. This is actually happening.

Magic—*witchcraft*—is real. And I—Sophie Stone—am a witch.

I am so not prepared for this.

Mr. Krueger's voice snaps me back to reality.

"Miss DeLeone!" he shouts. I turn to see him on all fours, trying to corral some zombie frogs into a box. "I don't know how you managed to switch the lab's frogs with live ones, but there will be consequences to your disruption of this class! You and your friends are in big, big trouble!"

Big trouble? I think. *You have no idea, Mr. Krueger.*

No idea at all.

13

A week ago, I would've been excited if Cella called and told me that she and Katherine and Devon were headed over to my house for a sleepover. But in light of recent events, there aren't three people in the word I'm less eager to see. Well, maybe Corey Upton, Ms. Lerner, and Esmeralda. But even that's a close freaking call.

You probably think I'm being ridiculous. And yeah, I bet a lot of people would be thrilled to suddenly find that they have magical powers. And maybe I would be too if (a) I hadn't spent the entire first fourteen years of my life trying to have as little to do with the occult as possible and (b) the magic powers I seem to *have* were in any way fun or interesting.

When most people think *witchcraft*, they're thinking of flying around on broomsticks, casting love spells and granting wishes, and turning loathsome enemies into toads. They're not thinking of having migraines, freakish accidents, and the ability to right a toppling pyramid of cheerleaders.

I mean, if I could turn Corey Corrupton into a toad, maybe I'd feel differently about the whole thing.

My thoughts are interrupted by the doorbell, which plays the theme from *Deathscapade*. Dum, *dum* dum de *dum*.

Most of the time the tune seems hilariously inappropriate. In Dad's movie, it heralds the arrival of a serial killer with lawn mower blades for hands, so it tends to make me giggle when, in our house, it heralds the arrival of Gerald the postman or a delivery of flowers.

Today, though, it seems all too appropriate.

Dum, *dum* dum de *dum*. Time to face facts, Sophie Stone. Go to the door and let in the rest of the witches.

"Thanks so much for inviting us over!" Devon trills loudly as she enters, sleeping bag and duffel in tow.

"Uh-huh," I mutter, but she ignores my negativity as she and Cella and Katherine make their way into the marble foyer. "Explain to me why you guys are here again."

"We *need* to be here," Cella insists. "You heard what Ms. Lerner said. If we don't work together, we'll never learn to control our pow—"

Of course, that's the moment that my mother chooses to swoop into the room (in her long, flowing skirt, she really does swoop).

"Working together is so important, I find! Hello, I'm Summer Stone. What are you lovely young ladies working on with Sophie?"

"School project," says Devon.

"Debate team practice," Katherine blurts simultaneously.

My mother's eyebrows knit together in confusion.

"Uh, it's a schoolwide debate that we need to practice for," Cella explains without missing a beat.

Summer, as usual, is too busy tending to affairs on her own planet to think too long about the contradiction. "Well, you can all feel at home here! And don't be frightened by me or Spooky." She winks. "Despite the human skulls lying about, we're a very sunny bunch!"

Ugh.

The girls titter politely while I roll my eyes with such gusto it feels like my eyeballs might actually retract up into my brain.

Mom continues on obliviously. "Our casa is su casa. And I do hope you'll all be joining us for dinner! We're having my famous eggplant tofu scramble surprise!"

Devon's manners are so good that I can barely detect her wince. "I think we really have to buckle down and get to work, Ms. Stone. We'll probably just order a pizza later, if that's okay."

My mom beams. "I admire your work ethic . . ."

"Devon. And this is Katherine, and that's Cella."

"Well, it is *so* nice to be meeting Sophie's friends at last! I'd wondered when she was going to bring you by the house. She's just been so private lately! That's how you high schoolers are, I guess. Well, I'll let you get to work!"

And with that, she swoops back whence she came. We tromp up the twisty staircase to my room in silence.

Once we get there, Cella flops down on my bed and Devon goes over to scrutinize my bookshelf. Katherine stares out the window at the sun setting over the beach. I walk to my desk and sit down. "So, let's get to work on that *debate project*, guys."

Devon giggles. "Smooth, Cella."

Cella smiles. "Hey, let no one ever say that I'm not a good liar."

"I guess it comes in handy when you're cultivating *magic powers*," I say snidely.

Devon looks at me sternly. "Sophie, I know this is hard, but you are going to have to come around to it. I mean, none of us are exactly thrilled about this development in our lives, believe me. But we have to figure out how to deal with it, and we can't exactly do that without you."

I just sit there sullenly. Deep down, I know that Devon is right, but that doesn't change the way I feel. I can't help but keep thinking that maybe I'll be able to close my eyes, tap my heels together, and find myself living my normal life back in LA.

There's no place like home, I think. *There's no place like home.*

I realize that I actually have momentarily closed my eyes. When I open them again, I find the girls all staring at me, clearly wondering if I've gone mental.

"Remember what I said that day in Strange Brews," I say, "about never wanting to be anything but totally a regular person because my parents are so, well, *not*? That goes double for being a witch. Triple. Quadruple. Quintuple. Whatever's after quintuple."

"Sextuple," says Devon, "but that just sounds wrong."

"I have to admit that I felt the exact same way when we started to figure out what was happening last summer," says Cella. "But we had each other—and it really helped, I guess, that we'd all grown up in Mythic, where everything's all about witchcraft anyway. And that we had each other."

"That's true," Katherine says, her brow deeply furrowed in thought. "But you guys know what *really* helped me?"

"Uh, what?" I ask.

"This." Katherine looks down at her shoes, and like *that*, her beat-up old Adidas are transformed into lavender-and-orange-neon checkerboard Vans.

I'm pretty sure Vans doesn't make that color combination.

I'm also pretty sure I've never seen a brand-new pair of shoes magically appear on someone's feet

Oh. My. God! This is more amazing to me than the winds that Katherine summoned to knock Madison off the top of the cheeramid.

"Whoa," I gasp. "Can you *all* do that? Whenever you want?"

"Well, we don't do it much because we don't want to make anyone suspicious," Katherine says.

"I mean, it is possible to have *too* many clothes," Cella puts in.

"Speak for yourself," I joke. Everyone laughs.

"So." Devon steps closer to me. "Want new jeans?"

I look down at my last year's Sevens. "Uh, *yes!*"

She doesn't wiggle her nose or wave a wand or rattle off any mumbo jumbo, but she does look at my legs kind of hard. And then I blink, and I'm wearing gray-washed, stiff new Chip and Peppers.

"These are awesome!" I realize that I'm smiling for the first time in who knows how long. The possibilities are endless!

"How did you guys figure out how to do that?" I ask them.

"The trick is to think really hard and get a clear picture of what you want. And voila! Or at least, sometimes voila," Cella explains.

For the next few hours, we play an elaborate game of magical dress-up. Maybe it'll seem shallow to you, but you know what? I'm sold. I mean, if I have to be a witch, I might as well be a witch with a high degree of style.

My first few attempts at clothing transformation go slightly awry—my jeans go through an unfortunate acid-washed phase at first—but once I get the hang of the trick (which basically just involves visualizing the item you desire, then concentrating really hard on the ways it does and doesn't resemble the thing you're wearing), I feel like I could happily spend the next few days just "trying on" new outfits.

My friends, unfortunately, have other plans.

"Okay. That was fun. But I think it's time we get down to business," Devon announces. She sits down on my bed, pauses, then turns slightly to face me, all seriousness.

Talk about bringing the room down.

"Sophie, I know you're not happy about your powers. But

there's good stuff that goes along with your witchiness," Devon promises.

"We mean, besides the fashion opportunities." Katherine picks up the thread. "We share something no one else does. It's ours, and it's our secret. I guess what I'm trying to say is, we may be different, but we're different *together*."

"And we'll always be here for you." Cella puts it simply. She rests a comforting hand on my shoulder. "No matter what."

I glance at each of the girls, take in their expressions. They're completely sincere.

When I came to Mythic, I wanted friends. I never thought I'd get them *this* way, but really, what's the difference? Cella, Katherine, and Devon *are* my friends.

And friends help each other. Even when they don't really feel like it.

I swallow the lump that has formed in my throat.

"Are you ready, Sophie?" Devon asks.

I give a small nod. "Yeah . . . let's do it."

Katherine cheers. "All right! Get out the book."

I reach under my bed for the huge volume. Standing with my friends, I realize that it doesn't terrify me nearly as much as it usually does to haul the thing out. I hand it to Devon, who flips to a page about a quarter of the way through.

"I don't think you'll be able to read any of it," I tell her.

Devon stares down at the page, confirming this for herself. "Hmm. Well, that's not strictly true. I can read it, but all I can read is the same old Mythic rule book. Sophie, do your thing."

I gulp—it's my first time "doing my thing" in front of an audience. In the distance, we hear the rumble of thunder—just enhancing the creepiness of the moment.

Outside, it's beginning to rain—again. It's another horrible thunderstorm, the kind where every lightning strike makes such a loud *crack* that you jump.

Judging from the coverage in the *Mythic Gazette*, I assume this weather—and the damage it's been causing—is part of the same system of "unusual" storms that brought my family here in the first place.

So it's a dark and stormy night, and I'm about to open up a magic book.

Cue the eerie music.

I flip the book open to a random page and, as usual, the page is blank. Beside me, Cella and Katherine gasp.

"I have to ask it a question," I tell them. "That's how it worked last time. What's something simple that we would want to know?"

I address this question to the coven, but the book responds. The letters slowly appear on the page, swirling and shifting, arranging themselves into what appears to be a list. A series of spells:

> *To call light to darkness: Lumino*
> *To bring an object to you: Propinquo*
> *To stop an object or person in motion: Desino*

"Awesome!" says Cella as I read the spells aloud. But then the book flips its own pages wildly.

Cella shrieks. Devon gasps. Katherine bites the cuticle on her thumb.

I stay calmly poised above the tome. After all, I've seen this before, and I have a feeling the book is about to drop some important information on us.

Once again, the book is still. On the page before me are detailed instructions for a binding spell. *To be performed only on Samhain,* reads the first line.

"What's Samhain?" asks Cella.

"It's the autumn solstice—more commonly known as Halloween," I tell her. Hey, I'm not Spooky Stone's daughter for nothing.

"Well, write the spell down or memorize it or something! We have to perform it, and we only have, like, a week to prepare," says Devon (ever the overachiever).

The second I finish transcribing the binding spell, the words on the page disappear.

We step away from the book, and each of the girls peers at the paper in my hand.

"This is really weird," Katherine comments. "Candles, yarrow root, *henbane?*"

"I know," I agree. Then I glance at the others. "Do you guys really think this is worth it? It seems like a lot of work, and I mean, what'll be different about us after all this?"

With a loud *smack*, the book slams shut on its own.

"Hey!" I squeal.

The volume opens again, flipping through its pages rapidly. It stops as abruptly as it began, and words begin to form on the page. This time, some kind of poem:

> *Be not fooled by fanciful things;*
> *The moment approaches, a challenge it brings.*
> *The legend is told, your destiny set;*
> *Fools are the witches that choose to forget.*
> *A coven that's bound is a coven that rules;*
> *You are the ones that evil pursues!*

I gulp. "Evil?" The book answers quickly.

> *Another like you. New to power, but strong.*
> *Beware . . .*

As the words fade from the page, recognition lights up Cella's eyes. "A coven is born every forty years . . . to protect the town from evil."

"It's the second part of the legend," Katherine says gravely. "The book is telling us another witch is out there. An evil witch we're supposed to fight."

"Sometimes the coven wins . . ." Devon says.

"And sometimes . . ." Cella trails off. She pauses, then continues. "The fate of the whole town—is up to us."

Okay, so not only am I a witch, but I have to save the town from total destruction?

Um, just a little question for the universe: Is it really wise to saddle a fourteen-year-old with this kind of responsibility?

"Hey, do you guys hear something?" Cella asks. She's standing by the window.

Katherine joins her. "No," she answers. "I don't hear a thing."

"We're spooking ourselves out with all this witchy stuff," I reassure them. "We're imagining things."

But a second later, I do hear something. It's a scraping, digging sound, and it's coming from outside.

Devon grabs my shoulder. "Sophie, did you hear *that*?"

"Don't worry. It's probably just the dog," Katherine whispers as the scratching grows louder.

"You guys." I gulp as I give them the bad news. "I don't have a dog."

14

Okay, it is late at night and someone is skulking around in my backyard. Our first impulse should be to tell my parents. Or possibly, to call the police. But what do we decide to do? Go investigate. Exactly the type of stupid behavior that gets teenage girls dismembered in every scary movie ever made.

Of course, the fact that we're witches does give us a slight advantage over the average Suzie Cheerleader. But it's not like we're good at being witches.

We silently skulk down to the kitchen. Once we make it to the stairs, we all freeze and listen.

The scraping/digging sound is definitely coming from the backyard, and it's getting louder, as if whatever's out there is getting frustrated or picking up steam.

Cella makes panicky eye contact with Devon, who whispers at her not to be a wuss; then we tiptoe en masse to the French doors that lead out into the garden. We're going to get soaked by the rain, but I guess that's not important. Not when you have a reincarnated, two-hundred-year-old evil stalking you.

A shadow moves past a garden statue on the right. A small, thin shadow. It's a moonless night, so we can't make out anything but a silhouette. And even that's hard to discern in the heavy rain.

"One person. Four of us. We can probably take down whoever it is out there," Katherine whispers.

"As long as he, she, or it really is alone," I reply.

We creep into the garden and crouch behind a hulking marble statue. The wind and rain are rustling the leaves around, which works in our favor since whoever is outside is less likely to hear us creeping toward them.

The eerie, howling wind also adds to the B-movie feel of the scenario. I may be slightly crazy for comparing everything in my life to one of my dad's movies, but I can't help that it's apt. I keep expecting somebody with knives for hands or a hockey mask to jump out of the bushes and say boo.

But instead, a flashlight turns on about fifty feet away. Okay, no supernatural beastie uses a flashlight, so we can cross that off the list. We peer above the statue we're hiding behind, but we still can't make out who it is beyond the bushes and small trees separating us. And that's when we hear it.

A girl's voice.

Chanting. Something vaguely familiar. Something that sounds suspiciously like a spell.

I'm getting more frightened by the second, and I'm not alone

hex education 119

in this sentiment. Katherine and Devon are doing their best to keep stiff upper lips, but I can see beads of sweat forming on Devon's perfect forehead, and Katherine is doing this thing that she does with her cuticles when she's nervous. Cella looks like she might faint.

I'm thinking that if she does, I might join her.

"Guys, we have to do something!" I whisper. But I'm met with silence.

Finally, Devon answers me. "We don't know what we're dealing with here, so we don't know what we should even ask the book. Let's just watch—and wait."

"Fine with me," squeaks Cella.

So we stand there, every one of our muscles tensed, waiting for whoever it is to make the first move. For five hour-seeming minutes, no moves of any kind are made.

Finally, we hear a thud. The flashlight suddenly goes out and the chanting stops. As does my respiration.

"Curses!"

Wait, did she just say curses? There's only one person I know who uses words like that on impulse and with complete sincerity.

I get up from behind the statue and walk toward the intruder.

"Wait! What are you doing! Get back here!" The girls are whisper-screaming behind me. But I ignore them.

I reach the figure crawling around on the ground, presumably searching for her flashlight. "What do you think *you're* doing here?" I ask.

Esme pops up and glares at me. She is wearing a black robe, made of wannabe-silk polyester, and has a pentagram painted on her forehead. In Day-Glo paint.

I feel the tension ebbing from my body—getting completely freaked out and then reassured should be some kind of new spa service. Esme, while a pretty obvious choice for the role, cannot be the evil witch. Not in that outfit.

She smoothes her red crushed-velvet skirt, clearly trying her best to look dark and scary.

"What I'm doing here is none of your business!" she yelps. It's like being barked at by one of those tiny terriers—the kind socialites carry around in their purses. Every second that I'm around Esme, I become less and less convinced of the possibility that she's a witch in *any* way.

"Uh, you're in my backyard, digging up my garden, so yeah, I think it qualifies as my business."

As Devon, Katherine, and Cella align themselves behind me, I notice the various tools lying at Esme's feet. A trowel, a couple of black unlit candles, a black velvet satchel filled with who knows what, a well-worn marble notebook with *Book of Shadows* written in Esme's angular scrawl across the front. And a broom. A clearly homemade, handle-fashioned-from-a-thin-branch broom. All she needs is a pointy hat and she really would be a caricature. I hear Devon let out a small, unladylike snort.

"Stand back!" Esme says with venom, picking up her broom and holding it out like a sword. "Or you'll be sorry."

"Um, is this a joke?" Katherine asks.

"I'm a witch, okay? So step off," says Esme earnestly. She packs up her stuff, glaring pensively at the ground. Clearly, she's seriously humiliated.

"Wait." I feel almost bad for her. "At least tell me what you were looking for back here."

"Nothing, okay?"

"Come on. Give it up, Esme," I ask, wondering how often she's been paying our flower bed a visit.

Esme rolls her eyes. "One of my spells required anise root, and I came here to dig some up. I knew it would be here, because old Mrs. Mulvane used to live here and she sold it every other week at the outdoor market in Montgomery Square. I'd order it online, but spells require that it be freshly cut," she says, throwing her root-filled bag over her shoulder. "Not that you shallow morons would know anything about it. And don't call me Esme."

"Where'd you learn all your spells?" I ask, genuinely curious.

"Why do you care?"

"Just wondering. And hey, you're the one skulking outside my house in the night. I feel like I kind of have a right to ask whatever I want."

"Well, I haven't always just worked in the Mythic Historical Society's Gifte Shoppe," she huffs. I swear I can hear the extra *e*'s in her pronunciation. "I spent the summer interning at the MHS proper. I studied all the ancient tomes of the native witches. They were full of all kinds of spells," As Esme warms to her topic, it's clear she's got no one to discuss all this with. Her eyes have taken on a dreamy, far-off look. "It was perfect timing on my part. Those books will be touring European museums for the next few years. Including all the medieval centers of witchcraft."

Suddenly realizing where she is and who she's talking to, she snaps out of it and gives us all a glare. She aims her gaze toward the moonlit sky. "Goddess, forgive these ignorant creatures for interrupting your sacred ritual. And please teach them not to question your powers." At this, she begins yet another incantation—one that sounds like a high-pitched yogic chant.

"Aaaay, yi, yi, yi, yi."

And then, with a last snarl in our direction, Esme slinks off.

"Well, I think we can cross one suspect off our list," Katherine jokes.

"Yeah," Devon agrees. "Except it seems to me that Esme . . . sorry, Esmeralda . . . knows quite a bit more about witchcraft than we do. And we're *real* witches!"

I sigh. Devon's right.

Looks like we've got a lot of work to do before Halloween.

"Ridiculous, right?" says Katherine, motioning to the cleavage-baring superhero outfit on the girl walking by. "What's she supposed to be, Wonderbra Woman?"

I giggle in agreement and wonder if Halloween is just an excuse for Mythic's teenage population to get seriously hoochied up. Even the Mathletes are scantily clad. They're all out on the dance floor wearing matching white skintight jumpsuits with lines and numbers written on one side. I think they're supposed to be . . . *rulers?* Jury's still out on that one.

I've always had an unfair advantage on Halloween: namely, access to the costume department of Stone Productions. I went with the no-brainer and snagged a costume from Katherine's favorite Spooky Stone flick, *The Makings of Magic*—I'm Malevola the Sorceress in a flowing, ornate black velvet gown and a long, glossy black wig. I decided at the last minute against the matching broom and hat. There's such a thing as too much irony.

Katherine is classily attired in black skinny pants and a stripey long-sleeve top. Her hair is pulled back, and she's penciled in dark eyebrows. She actually recognizably resembles Audrey Hepburn. Very few people can actually pull something like that off, and Katherine is definitely one of them.

Pembroke Mansion is the setting for Mythic High School's annual Halloween bash. The story goes—'cause when it's Mythic you're talking about, there's pretty much always a story—that Pembroke Mansion was abandoned decades ago and the house became the property of the town. But the town, busy with keeping up its more tourist-attracting . . . well, attractions, let the house rot away.

Then, at some point in the eighties, some industrious upperclassmen decided to hold a Halloween party in the old abandoned building. After all, the crumbling old ballroom and winding hallways full of dark rooms made Pembroke Mansion the perfect setting for whatever kinds of tricks and treats people could possibly come up with. The party was so awesome they decided to have another one the next year.

A tradition was born.

On this fine Halloween night, Devon and Cella are off flirting with their respective love interests, and Katherine and I are up on the first-floor balcony, people-watching. Before the party, we all decided that we would meet up at eleven and find a deserted room upstairs in which to perform the binding spell.

While I know that it's necessary, I'm still totally dreading the "ceremony" for some reason. I guess because it makes the whole thing seem so serious, so official. I look around at the party—everyone's dancing and acting silly in ridiculous costumes—and I wish I could be that carefree.

Katherine's hanging out with me since Jake left the party earlier tonight. Some sportsy thing about a big game and not wanting to stay out late. Otherwise, the whole high school seems to have turned out for the big night. There are a bunch of rooms off to both sides of the stairs, each of which seems to have been taken over by a different clique.

A drunken upperclassman brushes by us. "Heyyyy . . . something's wrong withispitcher . . ." he shouts, all red-faced. He stands between us, putting his arms around both our shoulders. "Two pretty girlsssnodrinks! Lemme getchua drink!"

Katherine pushes his arm off her shoulders, with more force, apparently, than Drunken Senior Soon-to-be Fratboy was expecting. He grabs onto me with both hands, his stinky hot breath brushing against my cheek as he says, "Heyyyy! Whaduyuthinkyerdoooin?" He's leaning against me with all his (considerable) weight, and I'm getting pressed up against the balcony. For a scary moment, I'm afraid we might topple over.

"Excuse me, sir," says a familiar voice.

The weight suddenly lifts off me. I back away gratefully—and watch Paul Pudnowski confront his natural enemy, Jockus Sportydrunkus.

"What'reyou s'posedta be, Pudder? Some kind of Superman or something?" says the drunk guy, pushing Paul's shoulder. Paul ignores him and backs away. He is indeed trying to be some kind of Superman or something, or maybe more like mid-transformation Clark Kent. His ordinarily floppy hair is parted to the side, and he's wearing square black-rimmed glasses. His button-down shirt is unbuttoned halfway, with a Superman T-shirt peeking out from underneath it. He's even wearing shiny black dress shoes and pleated brown slacks. Aw, poor Paul.

"You okay, Sophie Stone?"

"Fine, thanks, Paul. I—" But before I can even finish my sentence, Katherine grabs my hand firmly, pulling me away.

"We were just about to hit the dance floor," she says curtly. "Later!"

"Katherine, what are you doing?" I ask.

"That guy is *such a creep*," she says as we're walking away.

From the look I catch on Paul's face before I turn away, I can tell that he's overheard her, and I feel sort of bad. I give him a covert smile, and he halfheartedly smiles back.

Coven or no, I decide, I am going to have to set these girls straight about Paul. They way they treat him is just not cool. Back in LA, I probably would have treated Paul exactly the same way Katherine did. Huh. Maybe moving to Mythic wasn't such a bad thing after all.

Katherine and I head down the staircase, carefully maneuvering around couples making out and people heading upstairs.

Tonight's party could really rival any club in LA. Generators have been brought in, and the dance floor is filled with flashing strobe lights. Music pounds from enormous speakers, and on the second-floor balcony, where the staircases meet, the DJ has set up shop. He's playing a bass-heavy dance version of a song my mother loves, which should automatically make it uncool. But for some reason I am totally into his mix of Stevie Wonder's "Superstitious." Maybe it's my newfound witchyness.

"Impressed?" Devon asks as she and Cella walk over to me. Their costumes are, of course, nothing short of perfection. Cella's a flapper, looking completely different with her long mane up in pin curls and a dress that looks like it might actually be vintage Chanel. Devon is a sleek, gorgeous Nefertiti, with a headdress that looks like she might have stolen it from a museum.

I'm not sure why I'm surprised. After all, it's likely that some of this couture was conjured.

Devon grabs my hand and leads me into the middle of the floor. We shake our respective groove things. A few songs later, a clean-cut upperclassman comes up and starts dancing with Devon. She flashes me a smile before swiveling away across the room.

Someone jostles me from behind, and I turn around, hoping it'll be someone I actually want to dance with. Unfortunately, it's the furthest thing from it: Corey Upton, dressed to nauseate in a skintight red vinyl catsuit. Clearly, she's going for tired Halloween costume #1A: trampy devil girl.

"God, could you *not* bump into me?" she snaps. "You'll mess up my costume."

Yeah, what a tragedy that would be, I think, but I bite my tongue and move as far away from her as possible. She's got an evil smile playing across her lips as she dances—or tries to. Her costume's so tight that it renders all her moves jerky and robotic, and the plastic creaks with her every step. She's dancing alone, but her "seductive" gyrations seem to be for the benefit of someone to her left, someone toward whom she keeps glancing not so subtly.

I crane my neck to see who it is—and find myself making inadvertent eye contact with Linc. He sure doesn't look bad tonight, all done up as a James Dean–style greaser (if, indeed, his Levi 101s, white tee with cigarettes rolled into the sleeve, and slicked-back hair actually constitute a costume). Linc's band, Crikey Moses, made a special appearance earlier in the night, playing a few songs from where they'd set up on the second-floor balcony.

He gives me a crooked grin, then looks back at Corey, who approaches him as the DJ segues into a song whose sole lyric seem to be "Back up that booty, cutie."

I catch his look of resigned indifference as she begins, obliviously and creakily, to freak-dance, with her vinyl backside pressed against Linc's leg.

Looking at me over Corey's devil-horned head, he gives me a bemused shrug. Corey looks happy, but her happiness quickly turns to surprise, then shock, then rage as Linc backs away from her backside and begins ambling across the dance floor toward . . .

Uh-oh. Toward *me*.

"Hey, it's good to see you, Sophie," he says, talking right into my ear and flashing me a grin that's more devilish than Corey's entire outfit. When he moves in closer to start dancing with me, I make a halfhearted attempt to twist away from his embrace—but in the end, I give up. I catch a whiff of Old Spice and cloves, which smells . . . not as bad as you would expect. Linc maintains raised-eyebrow eye contact as we dance. I have to admit, he's not a bad dancer.

"I heard your band play earlier," I tell him. "You sounded awesome."

Linc smiles wider. His hands feel good on the small of my back.

Hey, it's a dance floor. I'm just dancing. No harm, no foul.

Okay, so there's a little voice in the back of my head that says, "What are you *doing*? Are you really dancing with another girl's boyfriend, right in front of her face?" I'm doing a pretty decent job of ignoring it . . . until I realize the voice isn't *entirely* in my head.

"What are you *doing*??" screams a voice behind me. Uh-oh. Corey Upton is standing with her hands on her hips, her face as red as her latex outfit. "I can't believe you're dancing with *my date!*"

Eeeek. Corey advances another step toward me and, before I can explain, she cranks her arm back and slaps me—right across the face!

My breath stops. Actually slapped! Across the face!

It doesn't hurt much, but I'm so angry that I stumble backward. And, of course, my heel catches the edge of my skirt, making a giant rip up the side of it. Also, my long, flowing, professional-grade black wig is lying on the floor a few feet away. The force of Corey's slap managed to knock it off my head.

I am upset. Very upset. And in terms of keeping the magic in check, that is not a good thing. I need to get the wig back on my head. Oh yeah—and I need to get as far away from everyone who witnessed what just happened as possible.

In one motion, I grab the fallen wig, which looks like a decapitated Cousin It, turn, and head up the large spiral staircase that Cella and Katherine climbed earlier. "Wait, Sophie! I can explain!" Linc calls behind me.

"Oh, shut up, Linc!" Corey squeals.

Ugh, they deserve each other. I run as quickly as my long, tight—now ruined—dress will allow. I need a place to cool off before I find Katherine and Cella.

The first room I try is filled with people. In the second room, a group of kids are playing some sort of drinking game involving relay races.

The doors to the third and fourth rooms in the hall are closed.

Hesitantly, I open the last door, and the room is, thankfully, a bathroom—an empty one. There's no seat on the toilet and no toilet paper, but the sink works and has a small, cracked mirror above it. At least I can reposition my wig and fix my smudged makeup.

My right cheek has a big red welt on it, and noticing this makes me feel blazingly angry all over again. I want to find my friends and tell them what's happened so that we can figure out how to get back at Corey ASAP. A massive public fart attack is going to seem like a spa treatment to that girl when we're through with her.

Fully repaired, I grab the doorknob, ready to head back out into the party.

The doorknob twists off in my hand. I push at the door. It doesn't budge.

Cue the screeching violins.

I have a bad feeling about this situation, mainly because, again, it's been in every movie my dad has ever made.

Why, why, why did I *not* ask the book for the spell for 'open sesame!'?

I'm breathing hard now. I have to will myself to calm down. Maybe if I just focus on the door, it will open. I concentrate on the closed door, staring at it hard enough to burn holes. But nothing happens. I must be too freaked out to focus my powers.

I kick the door. I throw myself against it bodily. I bang on it, hard, and scream for help . . . but nothing, it seems, can be heard over the sound of the bass downstairs.

Quick, what do the girls in the movies usually do next? I ask myself. Shout for help out the window? There is a window in here; I walk over to it, pull up the pane, and lean out. There's no one in sight—it's too cold to linger outside. I scream for help anyway.

No dice. I'm all alone.

Well, the coven will have to come looking for me soon, I tell myself. Though it may take them a couple of hours to search through this cavernous mansion, they'll definitely find me. Eventually. Well, maybe.

Gazing in vain out the window, I feel tears of frustration building up and sliding down my face. Just as I'm about to resign myself to the thought of spending the rest of my life trapped in a bathroom, I see the bushes below the window start to rustle. Someone seems to be climbing out a window on the ground floor!

I see one long denim-clad leg step out, followed by another. The mystery dude below dusts himself off and moves out of the bushes.

It's Linc! Apparently he's had enough of Corey backing up her booty. I swallow the tiny molecule of pride that I've still got left (it goes down surprisingly easy) and call down to him.

"Hey, Linc! Up here!"

The music from the party is still too loud for me to be heard. I silently will Linc to look up to this window, concentrating on projecting my voice out to his ears only.

"Hey, Linc! Up here!"

I don't know whether it's magic or sheer lung power that does it, but Linc stops short, his head whipping up to where I'm leaning out the window. "Sophie! You're not mad at me?"

"Your girlfriend just slapped me, Linc. Don't get your hopes up. I'm trapped in here. The door is jammed. Can you come up and get me out? Or tell one of my friends?"

He grins that crooked grin again. And then he does something completely unexpected: he starts climbing up the trellis along the side of the house.

Before I can open my mouth to tell him not to bother, that the door probably has to be kicked or pushed open from the outside, he's coming up through the window.

Well, great. Now I'm not only trapped, I'm trapped with Mr. Rebel Without a Clue, who is standing in front of me with one eyebrow cocked expectantly. "Well?" He purses his lips, and I forget for a second about the whole he-stood-there-while-Corey-whacked-me-in-the-face thing.

Then I remember it and glare at him.

"Well, what?" I say, trying to keep my tone casual. "The door-knob fell off and the lock is jammed. Someone needs to bust it open it from the outside. Now we're both stuck in here, genius. You pulled that little Spider-Man impersonation for no reason."

"I wouldn't say I pulled it for *no* reason," he drawls with way too much confidence. As he leans a bit closer to me, I catch another whiff of that boyish clove-and-deodorant combo.

Okay, I still feel a little bit attracted to him. But only a tiny, tiny, tiny little bit. Mostly I'm irritated. I'm dying to know why Corey said what she did downstairs. Could these two really be dating? The prissy overachiever and the bad boy?

"You're wondering why Corey slapped you, right?" Linc asks, reading my mind.

I sit down on the sink. "I couldn't care less, actually. She's just crazy." I pause for a second, letting the empty air between us gather weight. His cocky smile is fading fast. I want to torture him with as much awkward silence as possible, but my curiosity eventually gets the best of me. "Okay, tell me. What's going on between you guys?"

Linc shrugs and rolls his eyes. "Man, I hooked up with that girl *once*—at a party—the summer between seventh and eighth grade. We kissed, and that apparently means I'm her property for life. You shouldn't pay any attention to her. She's delusional."

"But you're scared of her. Why?"

Linc ducks his head, clearly embarrassed that I've called him out on this point. "Well, I know it doesn't exactly look good for me to be so scared of a girl. But Corey really is crazy. Like, has-a-shrine-of-me-in-her-room-with-pictures-and-candles crazy. I worry because I have no idea what she's capable of."

Yikes. That really *is* scary.

"Anyway," Linc continues, "she said something to me in the hallway earlier in the week about how she was going to this party. I didn't realize that meant I was her date or whatever."

I almost feel sorry for the guy—I mean, it's bad enough to be hated by Corey Upton. I can't even imagine how icky it must be to be liked by her.

"So . . . I understand if you don't want to talk to me," Linc says. "Any other ideas about how to kill time till someone comes to get us out?" He closes the remaining space between us with one step. He's just inches from my face now.

"What? No! We have to think about how we're going to get out of here." I brusquely push him away. But then, with zero warning, he leans back in.

"Trick or treat," he whispers, and next thing I know, he's moving in for a kiss. It happens so fast that I barely have time to process it. I get an overwhelming impression of warmth and winter fresh gum.

I hear a loud bang from somewhere, but I ignore it. Linc moves to place his hands against the wall on either side of me. My heart is racing. Oh, wow. Is this really happening? Is Linc Montgomery really going to kiss me? I close my eyes—but noth-

ing happens. When I open them again, I can see why: Super-Paul is clutching the back of Linc's T-shirt.

"What'd you do, Linc? Trap her in here with you?" he asks, his voice quaking with rage.

I put my hand on Paul's arm. "No, it wasn't like that. He was trying to help get me out!"

Linc pushes Paul away from him. "Get off me, Pudder. I'm outta here," he says, and stumbles out the door past Devon and Katherine and Cella, who are all standing in the doorway, their mouths agape.

"Paul Pudnowski," Devon snaps. "What are you doing?"

Paul stutters something about "trying to help" for a second, but faced with my friends' blank stares, he soon gives up and slinks away.

Cella is the first to recover. "Ummm . . . we were looking for you. Didn't realize you were busy with Linc, though."

Devon looks worried. "I've heard rumors about that kid ever since school started." She continues, imitating Ms. Lerner's voice: "Miscreant, rebel, and all-around troublemaker."

"Pretty much," I agree, giving her a wan smile. But I still wish the kiss had happened, in spite of everything.

15

There's no time to dwell on what just happened, because it's time to take care of something much more important.

We've got to head up to the attic and get on with the binding ceremony.

Devon leads the way, clutching a pilfered candle from the party downstairs. She turns back and gives me an encouraging grin. "I feel like I'm about to climb aboard an amusement park ride—scared, but in a good way."

I return her smile. Linc etcetera get further from my mind with every step. We're going to be an official coven. I try it on for size: "My coven and I . . ." "Oh, it's a coven thing." Not that I'll actually ever say this to anyone. Still, it's kind of fun to think.

When we finally reach the top of the staircase, we're so high above the party that the music below is just a muted roar, and the outside world feels very far away. We walk down a dark hallway, guided only by Devon's candle. When we come to the end of the

hallway, there's a door, which leads to another flight of stairs—just a few this time.

"Where are we going?" I ask.

"I thought one of the tower rooms would be the most private," says Devon as we enter the octagonal space.

I glance around the room. Windows on all sides let in moonlight, crisscrossed with the shadows of tree branches. I open my purse and remove the spell. Step one: sprinkle sand in a circle. Step two: uh-oh. We have a problem.

"I'm supposed to walk around the circle twice widdershins," I say to the rest of the girls. "What is 'widdershins'?"

"No idea," Katherine says. "But I can only hope that it involves skipping."

"It just means counterclockwise," says Devon. She looks super-serious and concerned.

"It's cool, Devon," says Katherine. "We brought the book, remember? If we have any more questions like that, Sophie can just ask it." She pulls the MHS rule book out of her massive purse.

"Yeah, and maybe it will even give us the answer," I joke.

"This stuff is not funny, you guys," Devon snaps.

"Hey, relax! I promise, there won't be a quiz later," Katherine says lightly.

It crosses my mind that, based on the legend, Katherine couldn't be more wrong. There *will* be a quiz—a very big, important one—in the end.

In addition to the book, Katherine removes from her enormous purse a small cast-iron pot, which she places in the center of the circle, and a few packets of herbs. "Whoa, you've been walking around with all of that stuff in your bag all night? No wonder you weren't interested in dancing," Cella says, smiling gratefully at her.

Each of the herbs, according to Devon's Internet research, represents something different: rosemary for friendship, henbane for secrets, yarrow root for loyalty, and aloe for protection. From a pouch sewn into the hem of my long dress, I pull out four different-colored candles: blue, red, black, and green. Nearly all of this stuff is courtesy of witchyways.com. It feels like kind of a cop-out—the book had suggested that some of this stuff needs to be harvested during the full moon or touched by the hand of a newborn baby—but we had it FedExed from a wholesaler in Seattle.

We're twenty-first-century witches, after all. I think we're allowed to take a few shortcuts. I mean, if Great-aunt Sophie had given me her cookie recipe, she wouldn't expect me to churn my own butter.

I distribute the herb pouches and candles among Devon and Katherine and Cella, and I keep the henbane and the black candle for myself. Then we place the pouches in front and hold hands. According to the book, this is the way the ceremony begins. We exchange nervous, goofy glances.

"You guys, we're really doing this," says Cella.

And then, in my most serious voice, I begin reciting the spell.

"I call together the four quarters."

Per the book's instructions, we then each whisper the word "lumino."

Instantly, the wicks of our respective candles flicker to life. Brightness fills the eight-sided room. In the center of our circle, in the iron pot, a small flame begins to flicker.

Well, that's pretty cool.

"North, south, east, and west." As I say the words, a strange energy flows through me. My skin feels tingly, but I'm rooted to the spot.

"I call the power of fire," says Katherine, and tosses a handful from her packet of yarrow root onto the fire. It flares up between us, casting a poof of reddish light on all our faces.

"I call the power of air," says Cella, throwing rosemary onto the fire, which momentarily flares green, like her candle. As she speaks the words, a tiny breeze picks up around us, whipping our hair and skirts around. The book sitting in the center of the circle now falls open, pages flipping furiously.

"I call the power of water," says Devon, and throws her aloe into the cauldron, where it sizzles and releases a gust of blue smoke. A gentle mist settles over us, then departs just as quickly as it came.

I swallow hard. It's my turn. "I call the power of earth," I say, reaching for my pinch of henbane and tossing it toward the fire. But instead of the cute little poof that the other herbs released, the henbane produces thick black smoke that makes it hard to see across the room. The floor trembles slightly beneath us. "Crap!" I say without thinking. "What's going on?"

"It doesn't matter—we need to finish the spell," says Devon. At least, I think it's Devon. Within seconds, the black cloud has become so dense that I can't even see the other girls clearly.

With my arms raised, I complete the spell, my voice trembling hard:

"Let the spirits honor our plea

And bind the four by earth and sea.

As fires swell and evil flees,

As we will, so let it be."

As I speak the words, the smoke intensifies. Then, just as quickly as it surrounded us, the smoke dissipates. The candles go out; the fire in the makeshift cauldron extinguishes itself. We're looking around at each other, speechless. The world feels eerily quiet, and I can't shake a deep-seated feeling of foreboding.

The book now sits in the center of the circle, open to another spell.

For Those Who've Strayed from the True Path

Night to day, day to night,
An evil witch is brought to light.
Seek the good, rescind the bad;
Relinquish powers that you had.

I read this aloud to the girls, who look appropriately horrified.

"Uh, what does it mean that the book is giving us this spell tonight?" asks Devon finally. "Does it mean . . . does it mean that the evil witch is here?"

"I'm not sure. Let's just go back downstairs to the party and try to enjoy life for a little while, all right?"

Devon shrugs off my suggestion. Cella looks like she might cry—again. And Katherine is busying herself packing all our magical supplies back into her purse.

"You guys, we should be happy! I mean, we're a coven! Yay!" I try to sound enthusiastic, but I'm just not that good of an actress. And neither is anyone else.

"Um, yay," says Katherine as she (with some effort) forces her purse closed. "Let's head back downstairs to normal-land—or what passes for it in Mythic, anyway."

As soon as we get to the bottom of the first flight of stairs, though, it's clear that something decidedly not normal is happening at the party. There's no music playing, for starters. Also, there's the distinct tart smell of smoke in the air.

As we reach the next landing, we hear the screaming.

"You guys . . . is Pembroke Mansion on fire?" Cella whispers.

Unfortunately, all signs point to yes.

Instinct takes over, and we all scramble wordlessly down the stairs. As we reach the second-floor landing, I'm assaulted by a wave of thick, chokingly ash-filled air. It burns my lungs in a way that the magical smoke from our spell didn't. This is the real thing.

For a moment, I'm scared to death, worried that we'll be trapped while the mansion burns down below us. Up ahead, I see Paul Pudnowski. He seems to be ushering people toward a different staircase. "Paul!" I shout. He turns and sees me and the girls. "Sophie! You have to get downstairs as quickly as you can. Take the back staircase—it'll be faster."

"What about you? You need to get out, Paul." He really does—his eyes are completely red and bloodshot, and he's covered in soot.

"No, I have to make sure everyone leaves safely . . ." he mutters. He turns to face all of us. "Try to get onto the back lawn. I'll see you down there."

"Okay, but be careful, Paul!"

Following his instructions, we hurriedly make our way out to the lawn, where the entire population of MHS is staring back at the house.

The spire opposite the one we were just in is engulfed in flames. And as we watch, the fire spreads across the roof. The flames leap and rise, devouring the old wooden building more quickly than you'd think possible.

The walls protecting the tower room—where moments earlier, we were all standing—are crumbling, about to collapse. The whole roof looks in danger of caving in. No one speaks—we're mesmerized by horror.

"The binding ceremony was supposed to help us keep our powers in check! I can't believe this is happening!" quavers a soot-streaked, suddenly very small-looking Cella.

"This can't have anything to do with us. Don't even think it," says Katherine sternly. I try to find her conviction reassuring . . . but right now, anything seems possible. And not in a good way.

16

Since Halloween, the halls of Mythic High have been a little bit quieter than usual. It seems like everyone has a theory about who was responsible for the fire.

The shifty-eyed kid who dresses like he's watched *The Matrix* about twelve times too many has had his locker egged.

The Wite-Out-sniffing girl in my history class gets weird looks as she walks down the aisle toward her seat at the back of the classroom.

And most disturbingly of all (to me, at least), Linc has been summoned to the principal's office, not once, but three times.

Gossip about the various suspects filters through the halls in bursts, breaking our self-imposed vow of semi-silence. I feel awful, and I know the other girls do too.

And today, as we sit down to lunch, I'm obsessing (again): What if we somehow, inadvertently, set Pembroke Mansion on fire with our magic?

"You guys, don't you feel like we sort of might have, like, an obligation to figure out what's going on?" I ask.

"Huh? Katherine says, looking up from her chicken cutlet sub.

"Well, there's the little matter of the spell the book opened up at the end of the binding ceremony," I point out. "I mean, a spell to defeat evil? What if—what if the evil witch—the one we're supposed to be battling—started that fire?"

"It occurred to me too," Devon puts in. "Though I have to admit that I've been trying not to think about it."

"Okay, I can tell you from experience how well that works. And let's face it—there's something bigger than random arson at play in this town. The weird weather that can't be explained? It's just been getting worse. We need to do something besides bespelling ourselves new footwear!"

Cella frowns down at her lunch. I notice that her eyes are bright with tears.

"Cella, look, it's okay that you conjured those Marc Jacobs flats last night. No one is mad at you," I reassure her.

But this doesn't seem to comfort her. In fact, she blinks and a fat tear creeps down the side of her face. "You guys, I have to tell you something. I should have told you sooner, but I had no idea what the message meant. This conversation made me suspect . . . Well, I should just show you."

Cella pulls out a small silver cell phone from her bag and flips it open, punches a few numbers, and then turns it around so we can all see. It's a text message, sent from a number that comes up as *unknown*. The message reads:

YOU'RE NOT THE ONLY ONES. I'M COMING FOR YOU.

"I thought it was spam! Like, promoting some lame new TV series about aliens or something!" Cella sobs. "But I think it's from the witch!"

"It's okay, Cella," Devon says, stroking Cella's back as she cries.

I notice that people at neighboring tables are starting to notice us. I need to deflect all the attention. "That jerk!" I say loudly. "How dare he cheat on you?"

Just then, the bell rings.

"We'll meet up after school to talk about this," Devon promises.

I stare at her in disbelief. "Devon, we need to talk about this now! That message means—"

"We all know what it means," Devon says, "but it's not like it changes anything, and right now, I need to get to class. Everyone keep your eyes peeled, okay? And practice doing stuff with magic that's more self-defense, less fashion-related."

"Okay," Katherine says.

I frown at Devon, but she waves my look away. "We're scared, okay? But there's no point in getting more scared. When you have a chance, why don't you see what the book has to say about all this?"

"Will do," I say, and we part ways.

As I walk over to throw out my trash, I realize I'm still totally fixated on Cella's discovery. There's definitely another witch out there besides me and Devon and Cella and Katherine, and she wants us to know that she knows we exist.

Why? Is she bragging? Trying to give us fair warning? I'm weighing the various explanations when I walk directly into a tall guy who's blocking the path to the trash can.

"Hey, long time no see."

Just my luck. It's Linc Montgomery. Before I can stop myself, I feel my hand reaching up to smooth my hair. "Oh, h-hey," I stutter. "You still on the hook for the fire?"

Linc smiles. "Nah. They figured out pretty quickly that they had nothing on me. The fire started near my amps. Why would I destroy my own amps? Seems like it makes people feel better to have a suspect, and I do a pretty good job of filling that role, usually."

He smiles as he says this last part, and then he winks—like, actually *winks*—at me. And he doesn't look cheesy doing it, either. He looks even cuter, if that's possible.

He *does* fill the role of high school bad boy charmer quite nicely, I think as I feel the bottom drop out of my stomach again. I try to think of something else to say to him, but I keep looking at his mouth and remembering our almost kiss and drawing a complete blank, speaking-wise.

"So, I was wondering if—" he says, but I cut him off. I've

finally come up with something to say, and I want to get it out before my brain freezes again.

"So how much longer are we going to be allowed to stand here talking before your girlfriend attacks?"

Linc rolls his eyes, clearly exasperated. "Now you see what I mean. She'll stop at nothing. She's delusional. Seriously, she's evil." His eyes dart in the direction of her lunch table, where Corey has her head thrown back in what legitimately looks like evil laughter. Some poor girl sitting next to her has a blob of bright red Jell-O on her cream-colored corduroy skirt.

Corey is holding the spoon.

"If you're waiting for me to disagree, don't hold your breath," I say.

Linc smiles. "My point here is, she's not my girlfriend." He breaks eye contact with me then, distracted by something behind me. "I have to go catch up to my man Tino over there. Peace out, Sophie. I'll talk to you later."

As I watch Linc's retreating back, I feel a weird mix of emotions. About Linc, I feel . . . like I'm developing a serious crush. About the coven, I feel worried and scared.

And a suspicion is forming in the back of my mind.

Is it possible that Corey Upton is seriously—*seriously*—evil?

I think I'll keep my momentary suspicion to myself.

For now.

17

Ms. Lerner is sitting at her desk grading papers when we walk into her classroom after school. She's wearing a thick, pea green wool coat and a pom-pommed hat—and yes, it's weird that she's sporting this ensemble indoors, but not because her style has taken a serious turn for the worse.

Apparently, the water pipes in the building froze last night—which meant no heat in school today. Yet another sign that the strange weather is causing this town to crumble around everyone's ears.

You may think I'm being dramatic, but put recent events together with the lore about the town being trashed by freak storms when good fought evil in the past, and it spells, *Mythic is in some serious trouble.*

Katherine gives a light knock on the door as we walk in.

"Hello, girls," Ms. Lerner says. "To what do I owe the pleasure of this visit? Come on over and warm yourselves by the space heater."

"Thanks. Uh, we're here because . . . well, we have a problem," says Devon.

Ms. Lerner puts her red pen down and gives us her full attention. "This is about the fire at Pembroke Mansion?"

We all nod.

"Did all go as planned that night? Was your binding ceremony carried out, as per the book's instructions?"

We nod again.

"So what is the issue? I understand that the source of the fire has been ascertained. A shorted fuse in someone's musical equipment, wasn't it?"

"That's what the paper says. But I'm worried that it's not the whole story," I say.

That gets Ms. Lerner's attention.

"Cella," I say, "will you show Ms. Lerner the text?"

Cella pulls out her cell phone, showing the foreboding message to all of us. Seeing it again gives me chills all over. I don't know what's scarier: the fact that there's an evil witch in town or the fact that she knows we're witches too.

"Another witch wants you to know that you are not the only ones?" says Ms. Lerner. She looks as shocked as we feel. Great. That's comforting. *Not.*

"Sure seems like it, doesn't it?" says Devon, sounding slightly impatient. "And the book knew about her before we did."

"The book . . . knew something? I'm sorry, I don't understand. The book is not an oracle," says Ms. Lerner.

"Well, you told me that the book is charmed to give me spells when I need them, right?" I say. "The night of the party, as soon as we completed the binding ceremony, the book flipped its own pages open—exactly the same way it did when it showed me the binding spell. It gave us a spell that neutralizes the powers of an evil witch, only seconds before the fire broke out."

I pause and take a deep breath. Cella twirls her hair around her finger nervously, and Katherine taps her fingers on a desk to fill the silence. Finally, Ms. Lerner speaks.

"I was afraid of this," she says. "When a witch decides to work independently of a coven, its powers can rage out of control—and without the guidance of peers, those powers can quickly turn toward evil. The time is upon us."

"What do you mean, evil?" Devon asks.

"Well . . . evil can manifest itself in many ways, but one of the most common is destructiveness. When a witch hasn't yet learned how to harness the powers, negative emotional energy can be transmuted into physical destruction. I have to admit, it has crossed my mind before now to be afraid that these storms we've been having, the town's increasingly dilapidated buildings . . . even today's plumbing situation . . . these may all be the handiwork of a witch. Every coven has a purpose. One of yours may be to stop this witch from destroying Mythic."

I've been trying to keep my cool, but now it's not working. "Ms. Lerner, what are we supposed to *do*?" I say, the hysteria bubbling out of me.

"Well, you must find that other witch. Any way you can. You must find her and, together, recite that spell. I fear that's our only hope." She shrugs and sighs. "For better or worse, you girls are the only ones with the ability to save this town."

Later, after we've said our good-byes and are trudging through Mythic's chilly halls toward the even more chilly weather outside, I feel literally burdened with what she's just told us, like there's a weight resting on my shoulders.

Just to recap: I've moved to a new town, found out that I'm a witch, become a member of a coven, and discovered that it's my responsibility to save the town from destruction, all in the first semester of my freshman year.

Instead of rushing right out to vanquish evil, I'd rather hide under my bed and cry. But I can't; we have to be brave. I just hope we're able to figure out who she is—before it's too late.

18

As usual, my parents have the worst timing in the world. I'm standing in our gigantic formal dining room, watching my mom direct the caterers placing trays full of fancy food—*organic* fancy food—on tables around the room.

My life is pretty much falling apart, I have to figure out a way to save the world (or, at least, Mythic), and my parents have decided to throw a dinner party. Well, a fund-raiser soiree to benefit the Save Mythic Fund.

Yeah, the irony isn't lost on me either.

On top of everything else, my dress kind of itches. It's velvet, and my mom bought it just for the occasion. It bears an unfortunate resemblance to the dress I bought quasi-accidentally from the MHS Gifte Shoppe, so good thing no one I know will be seeing me in it. Unless my mom invited *everyone* I know, which, knowing her, seems likely.

"Make sure that you have a few of the quinoa hash browns on each table!" my mom yells out to a harried-looking cateress. I move out of the way as she barrels by me.

"Oh, Soph, I didn't see you there," she says. "You look so pretty in your new dress!"

I make an effort to turn my lips up in what I hope resembles a smile. I'm not really in a smiley mood. And let's be honest, I'm lucky my mom didn't decide to sew my dress herself, what with all her newfound domesticity. I'd have ended up in a recycled bedazzled hemp bag. With fringe.

"Your friends will be here any minute now, honey. I'm just going to run upstairs and see what's keeping your father."

"Who did you invite to this thing again?"

"Oh, just a few people. I made sure your little friends and their parents were invited too," she says.

Yeah, right. That means that everyone down to the school custodian will soon be ringing our ridiculous doorbell. Good thing I'm too tired to really care.

I sit with a thud on the closest chair, totally exhausted. I've been up late all week poring through the dozens of books my dad has on Mythic's witchy history, trying to find some clue as to how covens in the past have rooted out the evil witch. Meantime, the weather has been acting up even more. Last week, strong winds knocked down power lines all over town. It took two days to get the electricity back on, and it's been spotty ever since.

The weatherman on TV has been talking about a storm system that's parked off the coast, gathering strength by the day. He warned that if the storm moves toward shore, Mythic will have to be evacuated—and quick.

Tonight it is, of course, pouring rain and crackling with thunder. Perfect party conditions.

The theme from *Deathscapade* shakes me out of my reverie.

"The guests are starting to arrive!" my mom trills.

Oh, goody. Time for some merrymaking.

At the door, we greet Cella and Mr. and Mrs. DeLeone, who appear slightly bewildered to find themselves dripping on our doorstep. Mr. DeLeone is a tall, weathered-looking guy who has *professor* written all over his corduroy blazer. Mrs. DeLeone looks exactly like an older version of Cella except with a sort of stern, regal bearing in place of Cella's endearing goofiness.

My mom is all over the DeLeones, talking a bunch of nonsense about Spain and aesthetics, which is apparently what Mr. D. is a professor of. As my dad comes in and greets her parents in fourth-grade Spanish, Cella and I walk on ahead to the dining room.

This is the first time we've used this room since moving in, so I'm not used to the high ceilings, antique carved hardwood paneling, and rich, lacquered maroon walls offset by a few paintings in heavy frames. The leaded-glass windows look out on the dense woods in the side yard, which are currently being pelted with rain. The branches are thrashing back and forth, scraping and scratching at the windows.

The golden glow from the antique chandelier sparkles on the long, enormous white-clothed tables, which are bedecked with crystal and silver. The only thing that keeps the room from being a total period piece is the flower arrangements, which look very Californian and even kind of match my mom's outfit, which is almost as loud as her shrill, high-pitched laughter.

"Nice decor," says Cella, grabbing a mini-quiche from one of the waiters walking by.

"Nothing's too good for the crème de la crème of Mythic," I say, rolling my eyes.

Cella and I huddle in a corner, and I fill her in on my not getting anywhere in the research department.

"This is sooo frustrating!" she says. "How can we fight evil if we don't even know who we're fighting?"

"Tell me about it," I say, equally stumped. "And the worst thing is not knowing what this 'evil witch' is going to do next. I mean—what if she outs us? Being found out has never had a happy ending for our witchy ancestors."

Cella nods solemnly. "Well, you know what? Let's mingle. Maybe someone at this party knows something about all this—something they don't know they know. Get what I mean?"

"Um, I think so! Okay, Nancy Drew. Let's gather some clues." We head off in separate directions to mingle—but not before joining our powers to turn a couple of the inedible quiches into cocktail weenies.

Hey, so what if we never manage to figure out how to do anything truly major with magic? At least I'll never be forced to choke down my mom's organic food!

People are milling about the room, some grouped together, chitchatting around the appetizers. I spot Devon's parents, who are standing by the windows talking with Katherine's family. They're wearing the kind of staid business clothes you would expect of two lawyers at the biggest firms in Boston.

Katherine's mom and dad are straightforward WASPy jock types—both sport outfits that they'd probably be able to golf comfortably in.

Devon and Katherine are off chatting in a corner near their parents.

As I scan the room, I'm reminded of the parties like this my parents used to throw in LA. Dad especially seems in his element at this kind of shindig—I spot him waving an hors d'oeuvre vehemently as he tells an elderly woman in furs and jewels a story that's making all the blood drain from her powdered face.

Similar scenes are taking place all around the room, and all of them fail to grab my attention as I scan the party. Oh, but wait! There's Linc. My stomach gives a little flutter as I notice how nicely he cleans up. He looks positively *GQ* with his hair brushed and out of his eyes. I don't want to get caught staring, so I abruptly shift my gaze to the other side of the room, where a tall blond girl is standing.

Wait.

Oh, no way.

Corey Upton is in my house.

Corey is smiling and chatting at Linc. I shoot my mom a

EMILY GOULD & ZAREEN JAFFERY

look, but she feigns ignorance (she's good at that), and I'm left to the always-inadequate guidance of Dad. He's now standing with a couple who I assume are Corey's parents. When he spots me, he gives me a jovial wave, motioning that I should join him. I smile, subtly shaking my head. Which, of course, he does not remotely get.

"Sophie! Come on over here! Try some of these delicious soy-cheese and bulgur mini-quiches!" He strides toward me, looping his arm around my shoulders so there's no way I can escape. "Soph, Townes Upton here has agreed to be a location consultant when I follow through with my plans to shoot my next movie here. The Uptons have been in the area for so long and are so familiar with its history, he'll be invaluable!" Dad says excitedly.

"Well, I'll do anything I can to raise the profile of our humble little burg," Townes Upton says faux modestly. He's one of those ruddy-cheeked, white-haired middle-aged guys you see so many of around here. His blond wife, who looks exactly like Corey plus thirty years, gives a condescending little smile in Dad's direction.

I don't need any magical mind-reading powers to know that what they're really saying to Dad is, "You're new money, and we're judging you."

Corey gives me a smug smile. She's looking, I have to admit, sort of presentable in a pink satin empire-waist dress. For once, her formal hair matches her clothes.

"Nice little place your parents have here," she simpers, fakeness dripping from every word.

Oh, it's going to be a looooong night.

"I just tried one of those soy quiches. Now I know why I always spot you over by the snack machines," whispers Paul Pudnowski from behind me. Even though the coven haaates Paul, I am grateful for the chance to escape the Uptons. I excuse myself from my non-conversation with Corey and walk over to a table with him.

"So, I haven't seen you around much. Not even at Strange Brews," says Paul. "Never call . . . never write. What's up, Sophie Stone?" He smiles, which makes the situation a little less awkward. A little.

"Oh, you know," I say, trying to be vague. "Hittin' the books."

Little does he know the main book I've been hitting is of the magical variety.

"Oh, man, I sympathize. Getting grade pressure from the parentals? You know I'm always available for tutoring if you need it."

"Thanks, Paul, but I think I'm doing okay for now."

"Well, you look way better than okay tonight," he says.

Uh-oh. Is Paul flirting with me?

"That's a nice dress," he continues. "It's good that you have some nice formal wear, because Mythic is all about this kind of event."

"Really?"

"Yeah. I mean, the winter solstice dance is coming up pretty soon."

"Huh," I say noncommittally.

"Yeah, some people even have dates for it already," Paul says awkwardly. I mean, he does *everything* awkwardly. But he says that last sentence, if such a thing is possible, even more awkwardly than usual.

"Wow," I non-respond.

"Yeah, so, well, I was wondering. . . ."

Oh God. I wish I could enroll Paul in Hint-taking 101. But since that's not an option, I guess I just have to go for the next-best thing: honesty.

"You know, Paul, I'm actually kind of . . . well, not seeing someone exactly, but there is someone I sort of . . . um, sort of have my eye on."

I don't know what I'm expecting here. Tears? Recriminations? Thankfully, I get neither. Paul chuckles, even though it does sound a bit forced.

"Hey, no big deal, Sophie Stone. Just don't forget the little people, huh?"

I smile back at him. "No worries there, Paul. The height-challenged will remain my pet social cause throughout my reign as Miss Mythic."

We both crack up at this, and all the does-Paul-want-to-date-me weirdness dissipates instantly. No matter what the girls think, this guy seems okay. At least he has a sense of humor, you know?

"Hey, Pudder," says Linc, walking up to our table. "Your mom was looking for you. I think she's over there by the spelt puffs."

"Spelt puffs? Haven't sampled one of those yet. Well, I'll be going, then. Have a nice night, Sophie Stone."

And with that, Paul walks away, leaving me alone with Linc.

"Was his mom really looking for him?" I ask.

"Nah, I needed a nice way to get rid of him," says Linc.

"I see."

"So what was Pudder going on about?"

Hmm. I don't really know how to handle this one. If I bring up the dance with Linc, he'll think that I want him to ask *me*.

Then again, I kind of do want him to ask me.

So, here goes nothing.

"Oh, he was talking about some dance that's coming up soon. Winter solstice? Sounds like a grrreat time," I say, feigning total boredom with the dance, the world, and everything, because that's what cool kids do, I think.

"Yeah, it could be fun, I guess, with the right person," says Linc.

One tiny butterfly begins doing laps around the inside of my stomach. I hope it likes cocktail weenies.

"Are you, um, going with anyone?" I ask.

"Not yet. You?"

I'm about to answer when I feel someone staring at me and look up to find—yes, Corey Upton—looking like she wants to pin me to a dartboard. I ignore her and turn back toward Linc.

"No, I'm—"

But before I can finish my sentence, a loud rumble of thunder sounds outside, followed by another and then another. Everyone turns to look out the windows as a giant bolt of lightning splits the night sky.

The music dies, the lights go out, and the room is plunged into total chaos. One lady shrieks, and everyone else murmurs anxiously.

A second later, the room is filled with what's got to be the loudest noise I've ever heard. This is beyond thunder. It's thunder's older, scarier big brother.

Light strobes and I catch glimpses of everyone's terrified faces. The sound of glass crashing fills the room, followed quickly by cold wind carrying tiny drops of rain.

Some *thing* whizzes past my head. Something heavy. And some tingly, unexplainable *instinct* tells me I'm in the presence of magic.

Then, just as suddenly, everything's silent.

"Everyone stay still and stay calm! The emergency generator will turn on within five minutes," announces my dad.

Of course no one stays calm, and almost no one stays still. I hear plenty of bustling around in the dark as people bump into each other every which way.

Linc and I stay where we were standing. I know this because as soon as the power goes out, he grabs hold of my hand.

I barely have time to find this cool or romantic—five minutes later, as my dad promised, the lights come back on.

Everyone gasps, and it's easy to see why. Our dining room has a new piece of furniture—a giant tree branch, which has crashed through the window, landing right in the middle of the room, about two inches away from where Linc was standing. A tiny bit to the right and that branch would have gone right through *him*!

My throat goes dry.

"Whoa." Linc murmurs.

The evil witch has just been officially upgraded from "annoying" to "potentially deadly."

It's time to go to the rest of my coven with my suspicions about Corey. We have to put a stop to this—whatever "this" ultimately turns out to be—before someone gets hurt. Or worse.

19

It's been a complicated morning.

The first thing I saw when I went down to the breakfast table was this week's edition of the *Mythic Gazette*. The photo on the front page looked eerily familiar: a grassy knoll overlooking the town. But the statue of *Macbeth*'s witches had been overturned, and the Weird Sisters were now facedown on the muddy ground.

The paper claimed this destruction was caused by last night's combination of flood-like downpours, which had turned the ground to runny mud, and fierce winds. But I couldn't help thinking our mystery witch was sending us a totally unsubtle message.

She wants to take us down. Literally.

It all makes sense in a weird kind of way. First the fire at Pembroke Mansion—after Corey and I had a run-in on the dance floor—that everyone suspected Linc started.

Then the craziness at the dinner party last night—after Corey saw Linc talking to me.

The text message also is *so* Corey's style—she is a know-it-all if ever there was one. The only thing I can't quite figure out is how Corey knows we're witches too. How did she figure it out? We've always been really careful to do magic only when no one is around.

But I've gotta hand it to her: Corey's perfect-little-princess image is genius cover.

The coven and I are now sitting at our lunch table, discussing strategies between studying for our biology exam. Yeah, that actual *school* part of school tends to rear its ugly head once in a while.

"Here's what I don't get. Why can't we just corner her and recite the spell and be done with it?" says Katherine, taking a giant bite out of an apple.

"Corner her where?" asks Devon, quite reasonably. "It's not like she's *ever* without one or more of her little pink preppy friends."

"Yeah, and it's not like we can all just leave during class to go do magic and not be missed," I say, whispering when I get to the *m* word.

"Well, there's always the winter solstice dance," says Katherine. "I'm on the committee. We're having it on the top floor of the Mythic Historical Society. They have a banquet hall up there. It's pretty cool—glass-dome ceiling and everything."

"Winter solstice dance?" I say, purposefully neglecting to mention my uncomfortable conversation with Paul and my resolution-free conversation with Linc. I figure we've got enough drama going on right now. "Is that like bizarro homecoming or something?"

"Exactly," says Devon. "We don't call it homecoming because that would be too normal."

"You know," says Cella, "I know that all fingers point to Corey and all that, but I still find it hard to believe that a girl who wears pink Uggs is a witch. I mean, how come we didn't feel drawn to her the way we feel to each other?"

"I don't know," I say. "Maybe it's because she's a bad witch? Maybe that's why we she grosses us out so much?"

"I think she grosses us out so much because she is a heinous human being," says Devon.

"Okay, we're getting off topic," I say. "Let's figure out what we're going to do at this dance."

"You mean how we're going to corner her?" asks Katherine. "Well, there's one person in the world we know Corey will do absolutely anything to be alone with."

"Linc," I say. "But how are we going to get him to help us without letting him know why?"

"We don't need to have him do anything," says Devon. "All we really need is to make her *think* he wants to be alone with her. She seems to like text messages. So what if Linc sends her one?"

"Steal Linc's cell phone?" I say, considering it.

"More like borrow it," says Devon. "If Sophie forgot her cell at the dance and needed to make a call, I'm sure Linc wouldn't mind handing it over. . . ."

"We text Corey, tell her to meet Linc in some secluded place, then we corner her and zap her—or whatever that spell does." Katherine says.

"Sounds like a plan." I'm actually sort of looking forward to this now. Finally, all the fear and weirdness will be over.

That is, if the four of us are actually stronger than Corey.

If we can corner her—and survive.

20

The weather is cooperating for once. Probably because Corey is happily looking forward to the dance tonight. Little does she know that her days of evil magic are numbered.

I'm not sure what to expect as far as the dance goes, but then again, this is the winter solstice, and this is Mythic—where every holiday is Halloween, a little.

The decorating committee has been slaving away all week, transforming the Mythic Historical Society into a set piece straight out of a Tim Burton movie. (Not that it needed much help.)

Devon and Cella and Katherine and I are wearing amazing dresses, of course. Even though the point of tonight is to catch a witch, there's no point in slacking off in the style department.

As we head up the stairs to the great hall, where a banner bids us welcome to the winter solstice dance, I notice trees all along the perimeter of the room—desiccated, dried-up Christmas trees with blackened needles that look like they were left over from last year or maybe the year before that. They're dusted with fake snow, and each branch is lined with Christmas lights.

In spite of all the tiny sparkling lights, the room has a creepy pall, which probably has something to do with the eighteenth-century torture implements on display along the walls.

Paul is hovering near the stage, talking to one of his AV club friends. God, he's such a dork—he actually brought his book bag with him to the dance! And his ill-fitting brown corduroy suit is, I guess, supposed to make him look like Wes Anderson—but instead, he just looks a mess.

And then, by way of contrast, Linc appears. "I wondered if I'd see you here. I mean, I'd hoped that I would," he says.

"Um, cool!" That's me, ever the queen of smoothness.

"So, do you want to dance?" I see no reason to say no. In fact, I've caught a glimpse of a super-styled head of blond curls in my peripheral vision—so I see *every* reason to say yes.

I'd forgotten what a good dancer Linc is. A few verses into a bass-heavy collaboration between Justin Timberlake and some lady, I realize what the unfamiliar sensation I'm feeling is: I'm actually having fun! So much fun that I can almost, *almost* forget what I came here for.

But a few songs later, I catch sight of those blond corkscrew curls again, bouncing annoyingly to the beat. I lean in and whisper in Linc's ear that I need to make a phone call and ask if I can borrow his phone.

As I speak into his ear, I catch a whiff of his clove-inflected cologne.

Whoo! Not. Getting. Distracted. Sophie!

"I'll go get us some drinks while you make your call," he says, heading over to the refreshment table.

And everyone thinks of him as a bad boy. He's more like one of those really dangerous-looking dogs that turns into an innocent little puppy the moment you rub its belly.

Not that I've rubbed his belly. But you know what I mean.

I head to the periphery of the dance floor and type in my message to Corey.

MEET ME IN THE GOTHIC GALLERY IN 10.
I NEED TO TELL YOU SOMETHING.

It's perfect. Vague enough to pique her interest, but not so sleazy she'd dismiss it as a booty text. Actually, what am I talking about? Corey would love to get a booty text from Linc Montgomery.

I slip the phone into my jeweled bag and head to the Gothic Gallery, where the girls are all waiting for me. We exchange smiles and slide into hiding places behind the exhibits.

Ten minutes to the second later, Corey enters the gallery.

"Just like a boy to be late. Liiiiiiinc! Oh, Lincky!" she trills.

Oh, ew. It's overkill—just like the bridesmaidsy dress she's wearing, which flares out in a fishtail train where its fuchsia fabric hits the floor.

Vanquishing Corey is going to be fun, actually.

I step out of the shadows. "Corey. Did you really think we wouldn't figure out that it was you?"

Corey's already-beady eyes narrow. "Sophie! What are you doing here?"

"You can cut the act, Corey, seriously. We know your secret. You are an evil witch, and we're going to stop you," I say, motioning for Cella and Devon and Katherine to step out of the shadows and join me.

"Are you all nuts?" Corey scoffs. "I don't know what you're talking about, but you really need to leave. I'm meeting my boyfriend here in a minute. And I think we'd like some privacy."

Devon shoots me an uncertain glance. I have to admit, I'm a little bit worried too. Corey seems genuinely oblivious. But maybe she's just doing an expert job at playing dumb.

We have to go through with the plan. One way or another. I begin the incantation, and the others join in.

"Night to day, day to night,
An evil witch is brought to light.
Seek the good, rescind the bad;
Relinquish powers that you had!"

"What the hell was that?" Corey asks, her perfectly plucked eyebrows practically hitting the ceiling.

Oh. Crap.

I look around at the other girls, who are clearly thinking what I'm thinking: Corey may be evil, but apparently, she's no witch.

I gulp. Well, I guess I have to do what I can to salvage the situation. So I say the first thing that pops into my head.

"Look, Corey, I tricked you into coming here because I wanted to ask you to please stop harassing Linc and harassing me. I really like him, and I'd like to hang out with him without having to worry about you stabbing me in my sleep." It's pretty easy to spin this out, actually. After all, it is the truth.

Corey looks around at us suspiciously. "What, so you and all your friends decided to gang up on me and—and *recite poetry?*" She wrinkles her button nose. "You guys are seriously mental."

I open my mouth, then close it again. Any explanation I come up with is just going to make things worse. In a situation like this, the best—well, the only—thing to do is escape.

So I motion to the girls to follow me, and we head out the door, leaving a very angry, very confused, very un-magical Corey Upton behind in the Gothic Gallery.

"I can't believe I did that."

"You didn't do it, Sophie. We all did," reasons Devon. "But yeah, I can't believe we were wrong. If Corey's not the witch, who is?"

We're sitting at a table near the punch bowl in the designated wallflower area, trying to figure out our next move.

I'm pretty sure what *my* next move will be: going home. The whole point of coming to this dance was to out Corey as a witch, and without that, the thing that makes the most sense is to cut my losses, hole up in my bedroom, and consult the book about what to do next. I'm not in the mood to party when I know there's a witch on the loose and I'm totally uncertain about who she is.

I tell the girls my plan, giving Devon Linc's cell phone to deliver to him, with my apologies. And then, after stopping by the coatroom, I head out.

The quickest route home from MHS is through the woods. I'm a little bit chilly in my thin dress and pretty but impractical winter coat, so that's the path I choose. It's a bright night with a full moon and a lot of stars, so I can clearly see the path in front of me. While I walk it, I try to piece together what went so wrong tonight.

All of the bad things that happened only happened to Linc. And Corey is the only person I know of who has it in for him. Are there any other girls who have crushes on him? Or anyone else he could have angered or upset in any way?

I'm drawing a blank, and I'm going to drive myself crazy if I keep thinking about this stuff, so to keep my mind occupied, I start humming a little tune to myself. "Superstitious," by Stevie Wonder.

So I have clichéd taste in music, sue me.

A branch crackles underfoot, and I jump.

But after a minute passes and the hockey-masked serial killer fails to appear, I chide myself for being paranoid and keep walking, humming my song.

I'm walking at a good clip, starting build up a bit of warmth when—

"That's a pretty song, Sophie Stone," says a voice behind me.

I gasp and turn to face Paul Pudnowski.

"Oh! Hey, Paul," I say, catching my breath. "You shouldn't have snuck up on me like that. You totally scared me!"

"Wouldn't want *that*," says Paul without a trace of a smile.

Well, that's kind of creepy.

Inadvertently, I back up a step. And he moves a step closer to me.

My heart speeds up. But wait. This is *Paul*, I remind myself.

Paul, who saved my butt on the first day of school.

Paul, who dressed up as Clark Kent on Halloween.

Paul, who, despite being a little bit dorky, has always been a good friend to me.

Fearing Paul is about as pathetic as being afraid of clowns. He's just a dorky loser. I'm not in any kind of danger.

So why is my heart still beating so fast?

"Why'd you ditch your friends?" Paul asks. "Finally realized you were fighting for the wrong side?"

I blink. "What are you talking about?"

"Being good has never gotten anyone anywhere. Trust me. I was a good boy forever. And all it got me was picked on or ignored."

"Paul," I say. "I don't get it. What do you—"

But I do. Suddenly, I do get it.

It's Paul. The evil witch is . . . *Paul*?!

He chooses this moment to lunge at me, grabbing my wrist.

"Let me go!" I shout.

"Not so fast, Sophie Stone," Paul says, a wicked smile playing on his lips. "There's the little matter of the prophecy to take care of, isn't there? After all, you're my natural enemy."

"But I don't understand," I babble. "How can you be the evil witch? You're a boy!"

"Silly Sophie," Paul says. "Magic doesn't discriminate when it comes to the sexes. And besides, I prefer *warlock*."

A stiff wind picks up, chilling me to the core. Suddenly, the air around us is filled with snowflakes. Not the pretty kind, the blizzard kind.

I'm too scared to think of the spell for "stop." Dessima? Dosino?

"Stop!" I say, panicking.

"You can't stop me, you silly little witch," says Paul. "My powers are getting stronger by the minute."

"Okay," I breathe. "Then just let me go and I won't tell anyone. Okay?"

Paul gives me a condescending glare. "I don't think so, Sophie." He doesn't call me "Sophie Stone" for, I think, the first time ever, and somehow that scares me more than anything else.

"I've known about you and your coven for pretty much as long as you have."

The snow is falling furiously now. The wind has picked up too. But I'm rooted to the spot—Paul seems to have frozen me in place.

"Okay, Paul? You're really scaring me."

"That's kind of the point, Sophie," he growls.

He paces in a circle around me. "I gave you too much credit, didn't I? I thought you were smart. But you were just like all the rest of them. I couldn't believe it. You went for a moron like Linc Montgomery!"

He laughs, and the sound is so bitter and painful that it hurts my ears. "But now that you know the truth, you know there are basically only two options. You can be destroyed with the rest of the town—or you can choose . . . to be with me."

"Paul, I liked you," I tell him. "I really liked you. It's just, I liked you as a—"

"Friend?" Paul bellows, raising his fists to the sky. *"You have no idea—no idea how tired I am of hearing that!"*

For a moment, I see hate flashing brightly in his eyes. But then he regains control of himself. His features twist into a hideous, grimacing smile. "Did you think I enjoyed being a loser, Sophie? Did you think I relished watching the girls I liked flirting with a popular idiot? The moment that I got these powers, I knew my days of being picked on and passed over were gone—*forever.*"

Around us, the snow is starting to stick to the ground. Ice is beginning to creep up my high heels to the backs of my legs, freezing them even more firmly in place.

I shiver. "Are you doing that?" I ask.

"Yes," he says smugly. "I don't know how—I just can. Like,

when I got mad at Linc and Pembroke Mansion burned down. Or the night of the dinner party, when the tree crashed through the window. I think of something—something bad—and it happens."

"The storms started this summer, the same time I felt this—instinct—to get closer to Devon, Katherine, and Cella. But they kept blowing me off.

"I didn't know why, and I'm lucky they did. They probably would have wanted me to do spells for rainbows and unicorns and crap. But the angrier I got at them, the worse the weather got. It didn't take me long to realize *I* was doing it."

He looks at me, gazing deeply into my eyes. "I'm stronger than all of you, Sophie. Can't you see that? Just say that you'll be with me, and I'll make you happy. Happier than you'd be with those little witches."

"No!" I shout. "Paul, let me go. You can't convince me to be your girlfriend by threatening me."

"I think you'll change your mind when you taste my magical kiss," he says. He begins to lean in toward me. "I've never done this before, but I'm pretty sure it will make you feel more . . . positive about me."

Oh my God, *ew*!!

I flail my arms, but with my legs frozen in place, there's pretty much nothing I can do except crane my head as far away from his as I can.

Help! I think desperately. *Please, help me!*

And then, almost as if they've heard my plea, I see Devon, Katherine, Cella, and Ms. Lerner approaching through the woods. "Sophie! Oh my God!" says Cella.

"The spell," I yell to them. "Do the spell!"

A chorus of voices surrounds me, and before long I hear my own voice joining them.

> "Night to day, day to night,
>
> An evil witch is brought to light.
>
> Seek the good, rescind the bad;
>
> Relinquish powers that you had."

Paul ignores the chant, but by the second time through, his grip on me seems to be loosening. Soon he's doubled over, as if I'd just kneed him in the groin. As he's kneeling on the ground, I attempt to lift my foot.

Yes! I can move again. Paul looks up at me with rage in his eyes. He's clutching his crotch like a toddler who needs to use the potty.

"What we just recited was a spell that drastically reduced your powers," I explain. "I'm no expert like you, Paul, but I'd venture a guess that your magical powers are now along the lines of . . . well, maybe you'll be able to light a candle with magic, but you won't be able to, say, change the channel without using the remote."

He groans and looks up at me imploringly. "Please, Sophie, give me my powers back. All I wanted was for you to love me!"

"Yeah. That was never going happen. And you really need to work on your approach."

"I'm not sorry!" Paul sniffles. But I can tell that deep down, maybe, he sort of is.

I turn to the coven and Ms. Lerner. They surround me in a giant hug.

"How did you know I needed you?" I ask my friends.

"The snow," says Devon. "When we saw the glass ceiling covered in it, we knew something was up. And when we couldn't find you, we went out looking."

"I can't believe it was Paul all this time," Katherine says, shaking her head. "I mean, he's a *boy*."

"Magic doesn't discriminate when it comes to the sexes," I say, quoting the man himself. "Apparently, witches *and* warlocks exist in Mythic."

"That was one fact your great-aunt *didn't* mention," says Ms. Lerner, looking visibly shaken. This mentor-to-teen-witches thing really isn't her strong suit.

"Let's get out of this cold," says Cella.

"At least it's stopped snowing," says Katherine.

"Yeah," I say. "Something tells me we won't have to worry about any freak storms anymore."

"So we can get back to worrying about the really important stuff," says Cella. "Speaking of, I bet that dance isn't over yet."

"Go," Ms. Lerner tells us, beaming. We leave Paul in her custody.

"Your mother will be hearing about this, young man," she says as we're walking away. She grabs his ear and pinches it in her fist.

"Ow!" he whines.

Nice. That kid is getting grounded till senior prom.

21

As luck would have it, we get back to the dance in time for one last slow jam. It's a pipe organ number, but hey, this is Mythic. Land o' the Weird. Funny thing is, I sort of don't mind the fact that I kind of fit in here now. Of all the things you can say about this town, no one can call it boring.

Devon dances with that cute upperclassman, Cella's with the guy from the soccer team, and Katherine and Jake look picture-cute together as usual. I'm standing by the wall. Just seeing the happiness my friends—my coven girls—is enough happiness for me. I don't need some guy to complete the picture.

I'm thinking this—actually, repeating this to myself—when someone behind me taps me on the shoulder. I turn and find myself staring into the baby blue eyes of none other than Linc. "I thought I'd lost you," he says simply, and without any more conversation, I let him lead me onto the dance floor.

As we spin under the ceiling of twinkling lights, all thoughts of Paul disappear from my mind, and all I can think of is the reassuring sturdiness of Linc's arms.

"So, how have you been doing, okay?" he asks after a while.

"You know, things haven't actually been that great, but I'm doing a lot better now," I reply.

Linc chuckles. "That's what I like about you, Sophie. You're honest, and you see things for what they really are."

"Huh. I wish!" I say, thinking of the time I wasted barking up the wrong tree, putting my friends in danger because I was so convinced that Corey was a witch.

"No, I mean it," he says, bringing his hand under my chin to make sure that I'm looking him in the eye. "There's something . . . different about you, Sophie. Something really special."

And then he leans in and kisses me. My brain is trying to think something like, *If he only knew how different*, but I manage to quiet it. Linc's kissing me and kissing me.

I realize nothing has worked out the way I imagined it would—but this moment is good nonetheless.

In fact, it's better than good.

It's magical.